IMPOSSIBLE JAMES

IMPOSSIBLE JAMES

IMPOSSIBLE JAMES

IMPOSSIBLE JAMES

IMPOSSIBLE JAMES

IMPOSSIBLE JAMES

IMPOSSIBLE JAMES

IMPOSSIBLE JAMES

IMPOSSIBLE JAMES

IMPOSSIBLE JAMES

IMPOSSIBLE JAMES

FUNGASM PRESS
an imprint of Eraserhead Press
PO Box 10065
Portland, OR 97296

www.fungasmpress.com
facebook/fungasmpress

ISBN: 978-1-62105-296-8
Copyright © 2019 by Danger Slater
Cover art copyright © 2019 Katie McCann
Cover design copyright © 2019 Matthew Revert
Edited by John Skipp

IMPOSSIBLE JAMES

a novel about death

DANGER SLATER

FUNGASM press

To my dad.

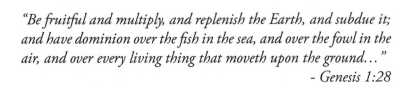

"Be fruitful and multiply, and replenish the Earth, and subdue it; and have dominion over the fish in the sea, and over the fowl in the air, and over every living thing that moveth upon the ground…"
                                                        - Genesis 1:28

"Every child begins the world again"
                                    - Henry David Thoreau, *Walden*

PART ONE:
CONCEPTION

1

The doctor had a big, bushy white mustache.

But that wasn't important.

What was important was that when he leaned back in his chair and held his breath, he did so with just the right amount of theatrical flair, the way he had seen doctors in the movies do it. Fade in on the scene where our protagonist had just been delivered some devastating news.

In the newfound silence that followed, the second hand on the wall clock seemed to echo like thunder against the indifferent walls:

tick tick tick tick

It was the only thing the two men in this room could hear.

Okay, so now a quick flashback. But only to a few minutes ago:

It was the same office. Same players. Same general atmosphere. But in this moment, and in every moment that happened to preceed it, the second hand on that wall clock lurched forward in the same sorry way it always had; unnoticed beneath the rustle of the paperwork across the top of his desk, beneath the rattle of his patients' phlegm-filled lungs, beneath the uneven beats of his own arrhythmic heart.

And the doctor sat there with his stethoscope around his neck like a fancy noose and thought to himself: *Jeeeeeeezus, dealing with these sick people all the time can be such a bore! WTF have I even been doing with my life?!*

Because you see:

When this doctor was a young man, many decades ago, he

had harbored a lot of unreasonable dreams, as did we all. These dreams often cast him in a multitude of more glamourous and creative professions. He would be a world-famous playwright. Or a bigshot Hollywood director. Or the author of trashy science-fiction novels. Sometimes, he happened to be all three. He would direct the movies from the scripts he adapted from his books.

If he could become a baby and do it all over again, he would've been a storyteller by trade. He would've told stories in any form, through any milieu, even if they cut out his tongue, however he could. His stories would've been crafted with such deftness and precision that they would elicit laughter, ignite imaginations, and inspire torrents of cathartic tears; his stories would've explored, in every facet explorable, the Unquestionable, Ineffable, and Unavoidable Truths that are Inherent to the Human Condition.

Holy fuck! Imagine it! He would've been beloved! He would've been great! Perhaps even the GREATEST! You never know.

He certainly didn't want to be a physician. He didn't want to define his world through medicine and science. He didn't want to be the ambassador of these fleeting moments, of this sterile office, perpetually the ward of all these frail and unfixable people.

But here he was.

The thing he knew was this: If you cure a person of a disease, there will always be another one to take its place. They're lined up, waiting their turn, like hungry transients outside of a soup kitchen. The human body was an incubator, after all, able to play host to a countless number of unseen terrors. Life itself was scarcely more than a series of maladies. Nobody escapes that simple truth.

BUT…if you're able to create something bigger than yourself—something like, let's say, a piece of *art*—and if that art happened to be transcendent and honest and true, well, then you might just luck out, and your creation may live on past your fragile, failing body. Your creation may live forever. Your creation might see the end of the world.

So that was why this particular mustachioed doctor could appreciate a thing like dramatic tension. More than appreciate, in fact. He *craved* it. He *coveted* it. Stories are built upon such moments, big and small. And when, in his capacity as a medical professional, he was forced to tell his current patient about his fatal diagnosis, and that shell-shocked man didn't immediately respond, the doctor realized what kind of scenario the two of them had inadvertently created, and he decided that what it really needed to put it over the top was some kind of symbolic gesture that could properly accentuate the kind of gravity they were facing.

tick tick tick tick the wall clocked then echoed, as we had established before.

Oh that's perfect! he thought.

And he finally exhaled.

2

"…so…is it…cancer?" the patient said, his eyes overflowing with tears. Twin trails of snot ran like a rivers out of both of his nostrils. He sniffled, but it didn't help.

The doctor was named Caterwaul.

The weeping, terminally-ill man sitting opposite him was my father. His name was James Watson. He is the main character of this book that you're reading.

"No, it's not cancer," Dr. Caterwaul said. "Though we should probably perform a few more tests just to be on the safe side."

They didn't actually need to perform any more tests. The results were conclusive. It just seemed like the most dramatic thing Dr. Caterwaul could say. That's what a doctor on the TV would say. And so, when it was his turn, Dr. Caterwaul said it too.

"More tests, more tests, more tests," my father mumbled.

"Tell me about it," the doctor nodded. "This parade of misery doesn't stop around here. You're not even my only patient *today*, and you're all dying from one thing or another. Every last one of you. I mean, I suppose we could send you for another round of bloodwork and a few more MRIs—but with such a limited amount of time left on this planet, wouldn't you rather compose a song instead? Speaking of, do you think I should get a karaoke machine for the office?"

"It's ironic," my father said, quietly. "So much can hinge on a simple test. Did'ja know I never got good grades in school? My dad always used to say to me 'James, you couldn't pass a test if your life depended on it.' Turns out, the old man was right."

"A karaoke machine, a smoke machine, and maybe a disco ball for ambiance…"

"The worst part was, I always knew the answers too. Sitting at my desk, those multiple choices lain out in front of me. A, B, C, and D. But something would go wrong between it registering in my head and my hand writing it down on the paper. It was like my wiring got crossed. Like I would short-circuit or something. Couldn't even begin to tell you why. Guess I've always just been a bit…broken…"

3

The sentiment my father had just expressed was not something new.

Hell, it wasn't even that uncommon.

James Watson's sense of self-worth had always been measured by a crooked yardstick.

School, and by greater extension the capitalist system that surrounded it, was constructed to reward those who bowed their way into the machinery, and this happened to be a particular skill set my father was not born with, nor ever learned. It didn't matter how smart he was, or how creative he was, or how many shades of colors he could see. It wasn't ineptitude that was his burden, merely left-handedness. There were rules in this life, and he was expected to follow them. This was the way of the world he inherited, the world he had not asked for, the world that spun around him and was spinning around him still.

To say it again in the most concise terms I possibly can: James Watson went through the majority of his life feeling and acting like an abject failure.

4

Of course, I have the benefit of hindsight.

I already know how this story ends.

And it doesn't end well.

I will tell you this, however, right here and now: if people would've recognized my father's potential back then, and if they would've fostered and rewarded him accordingly, I most likely would've never been born. Nor would any of my little brothers. These words would've never been written. And who knows what would've happened after that!

But honestly, it's waaaaaaaaaaaaaaay too late for me to waste your time by entertaining such useless hypotheticals. The second hand on that wall clock only runs in one direction, as Dr. Caterwaul has already illustrated. You can build your castle walls out of a lifetime's worth of *could'ves* and *should'ves*, and at the end of the day it will collapse in on you anyway. It's that same sad fuel that feeds all fires. If desire itself is scarcely more than a spark, what's an arsonist to do when everything around them is already burning?

So as distraught as James Watson was to receive from his doctor this terrible news, it was probably for the best. I suppose I'm just one of those silly people who believe that everything happens for reason. I like to think that there's some kind of omnipotent force looking out for us all. Call it God, or Fate, or Luck, or whatever.

Heck, even now I still think that, all these years after that particular doctor's office visit, all these months after my father's death, as I write these words while we're on the precipice of irreversible global disaster (a disaster for which I am most likely to blame) as The Gray Tide crashes up against our humble refuge in the Motherlove Incorporated building downtown, chewing support beams free from their foundation, threatening what is left of my tiny kingdom with complete annihilation. This is humanity's last stand against that eternal night, and here I am hoping for a miracle.

It's foolish, I know.

But like my father before me, I am a fool.

And I still have hope.

5

"So what we have here is a spot," Dr. Caterwaul said.

"A spot?" asked James Watson.

"A black spot, to be precise. In the center of your brain."

Dr. Caterwaul pulled out a large gray x-ray of my father's head and pointed at it. Directly in the center of two cauliflower-shaped lobes was a black circle, about the size of a dime, with tentacles of darkness veering off in all directions like rogue beams of moonlight.

"Right there," the doctor said.

"It's so small."

"Unfortunately, it's not small enough."

"It can't be that bad, can it? I mean, it doesn't even hurt…"

"Of course it doesn't hurt," said the doctor. "And it's not going to hurt either, unless it starts pressing up against the inside of your skull or spreading down your spinal column. Brains don't actually have any nerve endings, did'ja know that? All the biological safeguards your body has evolved to alert you to danger, and yet, I could cut a big ol' chunk out of someone's brain and they'd hardly even notice. That's why we don't put people under when we do brain surgery. Gotta keep them conscious, keep them talking, so if we stick 'em in the wrong place and they start spouting some gibberish, we'll know we made a mistake."

"So wait…are you saying you can surgically remove it?"

"What?" the doctor laughed. "Oh no. No no no. I'm sorry if it sounded like I was implying that. No, this black spot is not only permanent, it's going to get larger."

"Oh."

"Yes, over time it'll grow. That's how it works. It'll eat away at parts of your personality, piece by piece, removing all those little traits and quirks that you use to define yourself as *you*, until you're just…I dunno, an empty husk, I guess? A shell of your former self? A different version of yourself entirely? It's hard to say how it'll turn out for sure. It's different for everyone. But even now, considering its size and placement, my guess would be that it's worming its way through the area of your brain responsible for happiness. Am I right? Tell me, James, do you feel kind of sad?"

"I've always felt kind of sad."

"That's because the black spot has probably always been there."

"And you're saying this is…terminal?"

"Oh yes. Very much so."

Another greasy tear rolled down my father's cheek as he let out a heavy sigh.

"So…I guess you should just give it to me straight then, doc. How long do I have left?"

"Well, it all depends on things like your exercise routine and diet. You're how old again? Sixty-two, sixty-three?"

"I'm forty-five."

"Hmmm. At the black spots current rate of growth, and taking in your obviously declining emotional and physical state, I'd say you've only got about forty to fifty more years, tops."

That information struck my father hard. Like a weight had been tied to his heart and kicked off the side of a boat. His spirits had sunk to the bottom of the ocean.

Forty to fifty years was all he had left, and then, the irreversible and inescapable blackness of death.

That was it. That was all there was. There was no arguments to be made. No collateral to barter.

James Watson, my father, was going to die.

6

Now had this black spot first set its inky claws upon some other area inside of my father's head—perhaps slightly to the left, in the region responsible for fear—he would've been able to take his diagnosis in stride.

"C'mon let's fight this thing!" he would've been able to exclaim to the doctor, like his illness was nothing more than a parking ticket.

He would've wanted to discuss treatment options.

He would've begun practicing yoga, ate more vegetables, searched for and found inner peace.

Or, more magnanimously, as death loomed inevitably near, he would've set his sights on notions even grander. Horizons even farther. He would've gone out and truly *seized the day* in a way he had never seized it before. He would've booked a trip to somewhere he'd never been but always wanted to go, like…oh I don't know, let's say…Nepal. To the Himalayan Mountains. Sure, why not? He'd be a fish-out-of-water, a tourist, but not for long, and after a series of personal revelations and culturally eye-opening experiences he would fall in love with a simple yet sincere Nepalese woman. Yes, we are all citizens of the same planet, as James Watson would learn, all looking at the exact same scenery from a billion different angles, all searching for truth with the same beating heart. This was the meaning of life, in all its unadorned glory, and it was his to contemplate and hold in these final few days. His last breath would've synced up with the setting sun, a content smile on his blue lips, and when his body was finally lowered into its grave, surrounded by the hundreds of thousands of friends he made along the way, they would've all wept tears of gratitude and loss and said things like:

"Wow, that James Watson, now *there* was a guy who really had it figured out…"

It would've been a beautiful end to a beautiful man.

7

But alas, life was not a motivational poster that you could just hang up on the breakroom wall. And all of those aforementioned moments of spiritual illumination were not going to happen. Not for my father. And not in this book.

Instead, the black spot had besieged the place in his head where happiness came from. He no longer could feel any more joy. No more optimism. No more peace.

The only footholds that he had left were those hardwired deep in his rotten core, rooted in depression, desperation, and anger.

8

Perhaps that is the reason why, upon returning home from the doctor's office that afternoon, James Watson destroyed the kitchen table by hacking it apart with an axe. And perhaps that is the reason why he smashed plate after plate over the top of his head, leaving shards of jagged ceramic sticking out of his skull as he screamed so loud the blood vessels in his eyes all popped. Perhaps that is why he took all the food out of the refrigerator and threw it as hard as he could against the cupboards. Condiments in colorful splotches erupted throughout the room. Ketchup and mustard, gravy and jelly—a rainbow of soupy rage splattered across the floor like blood at a crime scene.

And then: he laid down in it, he laid down in the mess, screaming and crying, flapping his arms up and down like he was trying to fly away, leaving sloppy angel shapes in the sludge.

It filled him with unshakable fear when he tried to imagine how long that black spot had been lurking in his head, undetected. It was like learning that a squatter had been sleeping between his walls. It was like the ending of a horror movie. The call was coming from inside the house!

He wondered: was this black spot the reason things had never worked out? Was this the underlying cause? The source of all his struggle? Could it have really been that simple, all along?

9

Indeed, life until that point had been nothing but a procession of tragic doctor's visits.

We're jumping back a couple of years now.

We're going back to when James was still married to Petra.

Raven-haired and pyramid-eyed, Petra was his (then) wife and (now) ex-wife, whom he loved very much at the time, and whom he stupidly loved still. Even years after she left him, her name remained branded in his thoughts like it was cast there by a scalding iron: Petra, the purveyor of vicious love, the thorny rose, the poison cupcake. James Watson, my father, antihero of this novel, was once married to a woman who was better-looking and smarter than him by every metric one could use to measure such a thing. Her name was Petra, and she was a mean person, a trait that had never much bothered my father James Watson, because so many other things are more terrifying by comparison, and because mean love was the only love he once thought he deserved.

Petra wasn't my mother, by the way. You haven't been introduced to my mother yet, though technically speaking, I suppose I don't have a mother at all. It's a long story. Just keep reading, OKAY?

Anyway, it was from a doctor that James and his former wife Petra found out they couldn't have children.

It wasn't for lack of trying, of course. They had spent the first few years of their marriage attempting to conceive. They had utilized every third-rate fertility trick they could find on the internet—doing ostensibly insane things like wearing a moonstone amulet while drinking shark-penis tea—all in the name of bearing a child. These things, to no avail.

Eventually they looked into getting some medical assistance.

10

Dr. Caterwaul, whose mustache back then was just as bushy but slightly less white, sat at the same desk in the same office we had seen him in before, wishing he had a clock on the wall, wishing he had something that could've audibly *ticked* to fill in this oppressively-empty silence. That would have really driven home the magnitude of the news he just delivered this middle-aged couple. Really made it seem...dramatic.

He wrote down on his notepad: remember to buy a wall clock.

"What do you mean *infertile?*" my father said.

"I'm sorry, are you...asking me what the definition of the word 'infertile' is?" Dr. Caterwaul said.

"No!" my father shouted. "I want to know WHY *I'm* infertile!"

"Oh good," the doctor chuckled, wiping his brow. "Whew! I was like, 'shit, do I really have to explain where babies come from to this guy?' I mean, it's already awkward enough that I had to look at your semen under a microscope. It's like, hey buy a fella a drink first, amiright? I even got some on my finger by accident too. It was disgusting. You spend a decade in medical school and what do you have to show for it? A vial full of some chump's cum and an office with no wall clock."

"Doctor," Petra said. "What exactly are you telling us right now? That there's something wrong with my husband...sexually?"

"Yes," said the doctor. "Very much so."

"I knew it!" said Petra. "Even from the first time we were together, it was like *wah-waah.*"

Petra and the doctor snickered.

"Holdup now, whether I'm infertile or not, there's nothing wrong with me sexually!"

"Whatever you say, dude," Dr. Caterwaul mumbled. "What do I know? I'm only a doctor."

"I don't understand. How could this have happened?" my father said.

"Don't beat yourself up over it. Or beat yourself *off* over it, for that matter. Hahaha. I'm playing, obviously. You can beat off if you want to."

"What?"

"Look, it's really just the luck of the draw, Mr. Watson. Statistically speaking, a certain amount of people are going to be infertile."

"But why me?"

Dr. Caterwaul shrugged. "Not every effect has to have a cause. Sometimes the universe is cruel and random like that. That's just nature."

Of course, it's now painfully and ironically clear that the universe was already formulating a funny rebuttal to Dr. Caterwaul's lackadaisical explanation. Just ask me. Or any of my many brothers.

In the meantime James certainly didn't find it funny when, not even 6 months after that fateful appointment, Petra's belly mound had swollen up, ripe with the fruit of another man.

"Wait, what do you mean you're PREGNANT?!" James Watson said when she broke to him the news over breakfast. His voice was apprehensive. But also hopeful. But also confused.

"Are you…asking me for the meaning of the word 'pregnant?'" Petra asked.

"What? NO! I mean HOW! *HOW* are you pregnant? It's not physically possible. I can't make children, remember?"

"Yeah, I remember," she said.

"So was this baby immaculately conceived then? Are you carrying the Christ child?"

"Don't be ridiculous."

"I don't understand. What is the cause of this miracle?"

"It's not exactly a miracle, James. It's simple biology. Same as it always was, since the beginning of time."

"What are you talking about?"

She sighed.

"Look just because you aren't able to have children, it doesn't mean I can't…"

"But what…"

She raised an eyebrow and he stopped talking as he realized what she had been implying.

"Oh…" he said.

"Yeah, oh," she said.

And that was that.

11

James never found out who the father was.

A coworker, maybe?

One of their neighbors?

The postman?

The milkman?

A puddle left on a toilet seat?

A ghost?

All of the above?

Before the baby was born Petra moved out of the house they had shared on Sycamore Lane. She packed up all her stuff, every last item that proved she had ever lived there at all, and nested up somewhere on the other side of the city with her baby's daddy; a man who was James's undoubtedly handsomer and more capable replacement. He was probably covered in oily muscles, like he just stepped off the cover of a trashy romance novel. They probably kissed every evening, rainbows painted behind them, verdant forests and sapphire blue ponds and flocks of shadowy birds forever frozen against a golden sky.

Petra stopped taking James' calls and answering his emails, as incessant as they continued to be. The last he had heard, her daughter was on the honor roll at school, and that certainly didn't sound like any child of his.

12

Of course, not all doctors were the heralds of grief. There was still Dr. Anne. She was a very nice doctor, and a very nice lady. Not only was she going to quickly become a big part of my father's life, she was going to play a big part in the future of all mankind too.

But my father hadn't met her yet.

First there was this:

The month that followed James Watson's black spot diagnosis was a fitful month for the already emotionally-fragile man, marked by concurrent and successive episodes of emotional and spiritual decay.

The black spot squeezed his brain like an inky octopus.

There was lots of screaming at the sky and cursing at the god he didn't believe in. There were days where he'd gorge himself on ice cream and potato chips. There were days where he didn't eat at all, opting instead to lay on the couch and watch reruns of *Full House* on the TV set. Every time the laugh track erupted after one of the Tanner Family's terrible jokes it was like he was touching the void within his own heart.

He even attempted self-surgery. In the garage.

With a chisel and hammer, he bore a small divot out of the side of his head, lightly chipping away flakes of flesh and bone until there was a hole just large enough to dig his fingers into. He poked around a few minutes, trying to get a lay of his brain's topography, but it only caused him to do a bunch of random involuntary things like kick his leg in the air, blink a hundred times in row, and deliver a bevy of nonsense words with the magnitude of the Gettysburg Address:

"Four scones and rubber barnacles Agnes, our fork flagella gutter foam up grave dedication batty Arlo meningitis are coveted quails..."

When that didn't work, he cracked his skull all the way open with a good thwack of a rubber mallet. He slowly peeled back the front part of his cranium like he were opening the lid of a treasure chest. Pink cerebral slime sloshed out of the bowl of his head and ran down the bridge of his nose, taking the same route his tears always took.

Using a mirror he looked at the black spot. Dark, wobbly tendrils wrapped around his lumpy cerebellum, filling up the spaces between the wrinkles and folds. He tried to grab it, but before he could it wiggled away, burying itself in deeper. He tore chunks of his brain out trying to catch it. He dug through his gray matter like it was nothing more than sand on the beach, gouging out pieces and flinging them around the garage. The only reason he stopped at all was because he pulled out the chunk that contained his memory of the last 20 minutes and he forgot what he was doing in the first place.

He wandered outside, into his front yard, in just an open bathrobe, blood smeared across his face like war paint, wailing as dropped to his knees.

"Why? Why? Why? Why?"

Were any of his neighbors to look out their windows and account for it, it might seem like any other day of the week: the sun was shining above and the grass was growing below and James Watson was having *another* semi-public breakdown, as he occasionally did, and here they all were, together, at the end of the cul-de-sac on Sycamore Lane. James was having issues, but the neighbors already knew that. He had been having issues for quite some time. Since pyramid-eyed Petra was living there with him. And even before that. He had always had issues.

Yes, Brad Flatly across the way would think, as sure as the

wind would blow, James Watson would eventually be in his yard, screaming and crying about one thing or another.

But despite these occasional breakdowns, to my father, currently in the center of this new brewing storm, the day he received his death sentence was not like any other day at all, not like the time he found out he owed the power company an extra twenty dollars due to some kind of nebulous clerical error:

"Outrageous!" he had exclaimed as he climbed a nearby telephone pole with a pair of hedge trimmers, indiscriminately snipping wires. He ended up knocking the electricity out for the whole block for a couple of days.

"Worth it," was all he said to his befuddled and powerless neighbors after he shimmied back down.

So were anybody concerned enough to bother asking him what was wrong this time (they weren't) he would've just ended up screaming at them at the top of his lungs:

"You fools, can't you see it? Death looms ever closer! Its mighty hand is reaching out, not to offer me amelioration, but to take it from me! The clock keeps ticking! I'm going to die! I'm going to DIE! I AM GOING TO DIE!"

13

At a glance, you might assume this was a quiet street James Watson lived on.

Because it terminated in a dead end, there was no through traffic to come honking by to remind the residents of Sycamore Lane that they were still within the city's continued sprawl. From where he crouched in his yard—currently tearing up handfuls of earth like he were try to scratch an unreachable itch—the tops of the trees shielded him from the downtown skyline. An oasis, safe and suburban, tucked far away from the city's more dangerous and unpredictable neighborhoods. It was the perfect place to raise a family, if one were not infertile. The perfect place to build a life, if one were not dying. You might even call it quaint, were it not for the mostly naked shrieking man with the gaping, gory head wound now rolling around like he was being consumed by invisible ants.

Across the way were The Flatlys. Next to them were The Mosses. Everyone was in two story houses almost identical to his.

All the couples used to meet up and barbeque on Saturday afternoons: Brad Flatly and his wife Jennifer, Harrison and Tabitha Moss, and of course, James and Petra, the good ol' Watsons. It was a neighborhood tradition; a nice way to unwind after a long work week. Good times were had. And if "good" was too strong an adjective to describe it, the times they had were at least adequate. Inoffensive. Easy.

That is, until Petra left. Then the tradition continued as it had, except with James quickly taking on the role of a squeaky 5th wheel.

They didn't disinvite him from their get-togethers, of course. That would've been rude. And no one on Sycamore Lane wanted to think of themselves as rude. But his company became more perfunctory than pleasurable. Inescapable. A 'black spot' on their cheery suburban lives. And after the last hamburger was eaten and the last goodbye was said and the couples retreated back into their respective homes, wives and husbands would share knowing looks, hoping maybe James would sell his house, move on, move away, disappear somewhere, somehow.

But until then, James would always drink way too much beer. He'd stumble around, sloppy drunk, glassy-eyed and raw-throated.

"Goddamn it, my dick don't work right. I ain't got no jelly up in these marbles," he'd slur to whoever was nearest to him. "I'm shooting blanks." And then he'd point finger-guns at the Jennifer Flatly and go *pyew-pyew-pyew-pyew* like he was Gary Cooper at climax of *High Noon*.

"You've got to stop pissing in our bushes," Brad would say to him the following Monday morning as they waited at the stop for the bus to come and take them to work at Motherlove Incorporated downtown. "Maybe see a doctor, get that drinking under control…"

"I ain't seeing no doctor! No goddamn way am I seeing a doctor again. So fuck your bushes, Brad," my father would say, throwing his hands up into the air. "Fuck all the bushes in the whole entire world."

My father was not like the rest of them. Or so he felt. They were all perfect. They were born perfect, and here he was, this stupid crippled thing, limping by. He was unfixable. He had known this for a long, long time. And so he'd walk around like his skin was a Halloween costume, like he was just pretending to be James Watson, doing the things he assumed a James Watson would do.

14

He didn't bother to clean up the splattered food from the kitchen floor and it started to rot. Mold consumed it in a creeping, green wave. It putrefied and stank. The smell didn't affect my father though. Either he had grown used to it, or he just didn't care. He had stopped showering too.

It was the middle of the afternoon, a week after his meltdown in the front yard. He hadn't left the house since then. The blinds were closed. No sunlight could get through. He was passed out on the linoleum floor. Cockroaches and maggots writhed around his head, like a halo.

His cellphone eventually rang, though, and his eyes opened like they needed to be oiled. Without bothering to sit up he hit the answer button, leaving a greasy fingerprint on the screen.

"Hello?" James Watson gurgled into the receiver. His throat was dry and his voice was hoarse. He hadn't spoken to anyone in days.

"James?" the man on the phone said. "What are you doing?! Where the hell are you?!"

"Who is this?"

"What are you talking about? It's Brad…"

James said nothing.

"Brad Flatly. Your neighbor. And co-worker."

James still said nothing.

"C'mon man…"

"You come on."

"I've lived next door to you for the past 10 years. You pissed in my bushes last week and wouldn't stop talking to my wife about your low sperm count..."

"Oh right," said James. "Brad Flatly, yes, my neighbor and co-worker, how could I forget? Sperm count is still non-existent, in case the missus was wondering."

"She—"

"Hey, how'd you get my number anyway?"

"How'd I get your -- Jesus, man, are you drunk right now?"

"I was actually sleeping *off* my drunkenness from yesterday, if that's alright with you, *Brad*. Any more questions, or can I go?"

"Look, James, I'm calling to give you a heads-up: they're doing performance reviews today. Haggerty is on the warpath and you haven't been to the office in 6 days."

"Give me a break, okay Brad? I've just been diagnosed with a fatal disease. I've got a lot on my plate right now and I really need to just sleep some more..."

James nestled back into the rotten food. It squished up around him, soft and warm, like a hug from a lover.

"Wait, *what*?" Brad Flatly said after a slight pause.

"Oh yeah. I hadn't told you yet. I have a fatal disease. Turns out there's black spot on my brain and it's going to kill me. I've lived a short and ultimately meaningless life, and now, I'm going to die, and there will be no proof, no markers left on this ugly planet to let anyone know that I even existed at all. It is the true face of unimaginable cosmic horror, Brad, one that you'd be able to see is your future too if you weren't so blithely and intentionally utilizing all your dwindling time trying to ignore it."

"James—I—I don't know what to say..."

"What can one say when confronted with the irrevocable certainty of their own doom?"

"This is some heavy news."

"It sure fucking is," James said.

"How—um...if you don't mind my asking—how long did they say you have left?"

"Hard to say, Brad. These kindsa things are unpredictable, ya know? I mean, I could die today if I really tried. But the doctor gave me fifty more years, tops."

There was another pause.

"Fifty years?" Brad Flatly said…flatly.

"Yeah."

"I mean…that kinda leaves you with enough time to get down here for your review then, right?"

15

James eventually made it into work.

He hopped on the late bus out of Sycamore Lane. He was the only one on it. Nobody rode the late bus. The driver gave him a harried glance as he scuttled on, the stench of garbage trailing closely behind. They didn't talk. The radio didn't play.

James Watson was still in his bathrobe when he arrived downtown. Spoiled food caked in his hair. Unshaven and unkempt. When he stepped off the elevator and onto Motherlove Incorporated's main office floor the people nearest to him stopped and stared. They murmured amongst themselves. Gossip, gossip, gossip. And yet, they suddenly became very interested in the copy machine, or enthralled in a blank email page, whenever my father's bloodshot eyes rolled heavily their way.

Brad Flatly poked his head up out of his cubicle and spotted James. He fast-walked over to his disheveled neighbor.

"There you are!" said Brad.

"Yes yes, here I am," my father replied, throwing his arms up in the air. "Plucked out the sky like I was god's special little banana, and delivered right to your doorstep."

"Good god, James, you look and smell like dog shit."

"I couldn't find my tie…"

"Go clean yourself up in the bathroom or something. Haggerty is looking for you."

"Well I wouldn't want to keep Mr. Haggerty waiting,

would I?" James said. "The sun would surely stop burning were Mr. Haggerty forced to sit there on his fat ass for an extra five fucking seconds…"

James walked away from Brad, but he didn't go clean himself up in the bathroom. Instead, he peeled off a putrid garlic clove that had been stuck to his belly and ate it raw. His breath felt like acid in his cheeks every time he exhaled.

16

The company James Watson worked for was called Motherlove Incorporated.

Many years later, I would end up working for them too. I work for them now.

Like father, like son.

Like everyone else.

To quote from the top of their Wiki page:

"Motherlove Goods & Services Inc. [listed MLGS on the NASDAQ] is a multinational electronic commerce and computing company founded in 2005 and is the largest internet-based retailer in the world by total sales and market capitalization."

A perfunctory and sterile descriptor, I know I know, but like I said, I pulled this from Wikipedia, not out of *Wuthering Heights*.

If you really wanted to chronicle—in any kind of satisfactory detail—the type of business that Motherlove Incorporated *actually* did, it would take an entire almanac unto its own. Their investments were as copious as they were varied, and I don't have the patience (nor I the space on this page) to categorize and catalog every little economic detail for you. Like we don't have bigger fish to fry at this point. Take a look outside: the world is ending, and not in the metaphorical, hyperbolized, or abstract sense of the word, but in a very real and immediate way. I told you this before, The Gray Tide is here, and it is consuming everything it touches. There is no bargaining with it, and there is no escaping it either. And so this book will probably be the last manuscript anyone ever writes.

Revelations. Humankind's last gasp, as useless as last gasps are. Don't you get it yet? This isn't a biography. It's a fucking eulogy. You think I want to waste all my last breaths talking about TPS reports?

But in case you're just waking up from a thirty-year coma, groggily wondering the who-what-where-when-and-why of it all, let quickly summarize it for you so we can move on: Motherlove Incorporated mainly dealt in the data sector, first as an online retailer, and later, as a massive distribution and logistics corporation so large they basically became their own self-sustaining economy. As their capital grew over the past few years, they've acquired additional branches in every other industrial field you could possibly name, both in cyber and physical space: manufacturing, real estate, news media, advertising, pharmaceuticals, agriculture, transportation, aeronautics, and so on and so on. Nowadays there wasn't a honeypot they didn't have their sticky fingers in.

But I don't have to tell you this.

You know Motherlove Incorporated.

EVERYONE knows Motherlove Incorporated.

You probably bought the last book you read though their website using the operating system powered by their software on the phone that was built in one of their factories. And the groceries they surely delivered to your front door were grown on the farms that they owned with the genetically modified seeds they developed and trademarked. And, of course, as the largest employer in the city, statistically speaking, you were probably already working for them in some capacity, collecting the paycheck you will fed right back to them as you carved out the hovel you called home, thus closing the loop between consumerism and commerce, with Motherlove at the top.

They were a mega-conglomerate. The biggest and most-successful of their kind. The type of company that, were this book like every other a dystopian sci-fi novel to ever be written, would be the BIG, BAD GUY:

Of course they're evil, you in the knowing, entertainment-savvy audience would say, *what type of non-evil company would call themselves Motherlove anyway?*

17

Nevertheless, the particular office James Watson worked at was located inside Motherlove Incorporated's headquarters, an imposing and crooked building that cast its imposing and crooked shadow over the east end of downtown.

James stood in center of the massive main open floor like a pebble of sand on a limitless beach. The room around him was cast to four corners that were not there. There were no corners in this room. There were no walls either. The office spread out, infinitely large, around him.

And before you can ask:

Calling the Motherlove office 'infinitely large' is not an exaggerated statement on my behalf. I know it must sound like it, but it is not. I am not trying to conjure up an image in your head of a towering, warehouse-like room—with neon lights lining cathedral ceilings, crisscrossed by a patchwork of metal beams—under which a slew of nameless peons do nameless work for the soul-crushing corporate machine, although that indeed was what was happening.

And I'm certainly not implying that the office just *appeared* to be infinitely large from James Watson's narrow perspective, though technically, I suppose that was true too.

When I say that the room around him was INFINITELY LARGE I mean that, quite literally, the main floor of this office existed in a perpetual state that had no borders, sprawling outward in every direction before eventually succumbing to the tyranny of opposing horizons. It was like outer space, baby! It just went on and on! To gaze upon it was to gaze upon the ocean for the first time, as if wherever you stood made you a castaway, an island. It was an endless expanse, an incomprehensible enclosure; this office's size was limited only by the scope of human imagination.

The employees scarcely noticed because they had work to do, but it boggled the mind to try and take it all in.

In logical sense, it shouldn't exist. And yet, it did.

It was a feat known in the design world as The Impossible Room.

18

In a 2009 interview in *Newsweek*, the architect of the Motherlove Building, a half-Norwegian expat named Einar Kjølaas, was asked how he constructed a room that seemingly defied the laws of physics. To answer this, the interviewer noted, the slender architect lit up a cigarette before replying: "First, I designed a very large room. The largest I could think of. Then I designed a room even larger than that. And when I was done, I designed one again, this time even larger than all those that had come before. All one needs to do to pursue such an enterprise is follow this line of thinking to its interminable end."

19

So all of the husbands and all of the wives who lived on the cul-de-sac at the end of Sycamore Lane also worked in the Motherlove Building. Like I told you before, almost all of the people who lived in the city either worked in this office or *for* this office. Even my father's ex-wife Petra was in here, somewhere, in The Impossible Room, and presumably so was her baby's daddy too – the mystery man who impregnated her with the joy and ease in which James could not.

Cubicles like honeycombs zigzagged about, left and right. Maneuvering around them was a disorienting task. They branched chaotically, like pulmonary veins throughout the room. The mailpeople and coffee-gofers walked miles and miles each day. Without waypoints, without the aid of windows or skylights, knowing where you were in relationship to everything else was nearly hopeless. It was not unlike wandering lost through a casino. Finding the elevator down to the lobby so you could go home in the evening was usually pure chance.

If James knew where Petra's desk was located in this corporate labyrinth, he might've tried to do something to try and woo her back. Mean love was better than no love at all. He might've hired a mariachi band and sent them over to serenade her. Or he might've dug a tunnel from under his desk to hers, and then popped up like a jack-in-the-box, holding a dozen roses. Or heck, if that didn't work, he might've learned to fly a Martin B-57 jet and then firebombed this whole building to hell, leaving a steaming crater in the center of the city, screaming "if I can't have you, no one can!"

If we're talking "might'ves" the possibilities were endless.

What he actually *did*, and actually *had done* for the past few years, was to simply write Petra short, pathetic, impassioned messages, which he'd send to her daily through the intraoffice mailing system. He'd just click send and blast his misplaced affections out into cyberspace. Stuff like:

"Since you've been gone my entire life has become a blur. Sometimes I don't even know what year it is. Sometimes I don't know if it's day time or night time. Sometimes, when I wake up in the morning, I'll forget to open my eyes and I'll blindly stumble around the house calling out your name..."

—and—

"I can't help the fact that biology has decided to rob me of my reproductive functions. There's ways around this. We can always get a cat. And we can shove the cat up your vagina so you can give birth to it later. We can get 31 cats, if you want. Would that make you happy? A newborn cat for every day of the month..."

—and—

"I'll help you raise that other man's baby. I'll raise all his babies, even the one's he had before he met you. Heck, if he wants to jerk off on my tongue while you watch, I'll let him do it. It doesn't matter, just PLEASE Petra, I'm so alone..."

She'd never respond to these letters, of course. What kind of response is appropriate when your ex-husband is offering to let your baby's daddy masturbate into his mouth? She ignored his barrage of messages for years, until she got the one that told her about the black spot on his brain.

"I'm dying," was all his message succinctly said.

To which she finally wrote back, telling him outright what her silence was merely suggesting before:

"I don't care."

20

"So there you are, Watson," Mr. Haggerty said, laying his swollen palm on my father's shoulder.

James spun around and forced a broken smile across his face. Haggerty's nostrils flared with disgust as he eyeballed his ragged employee. "Jesus Christ, what is going on with you? You're covered in garbage! And is that a bathrobe you're wearing? I can see your testicles. Where is your tie?"

"I forgot the tie at home," said James. "I've had a rough morning."

"I can tell," Haggerty snorted. "Well this review shouldn't take long. Follow me, please…"

And the two of them slipped off into Mr. Haggerty's private office area.

21

Mr. Haggerty was an egg of a man, white and round and fragile and smooth, stuffed into a suit that fit even tighter than his skin. Hair grease ran down his brow and errant teeth filled up the space between his lips. He was full of butter and rage, the type of man who always appeared to be showing the early symptoms of cardiac arrest, exuding sweat from his pores the way a lothario exuded pheromones. Yet he, like I, like all of us, went through his days pretending like everything was fine, as if death would never come. As if he was going to live forever.

"Go ahead and take a seat, Watson."

He motioned with a trembling hand for my father to sit down. There was no chair where he was pointing though. Aside from Haggerty's desk, the room was completely empty.

"A seat?"

"Is there a problem?" Mr. Haggerty said, raising an eyebrow.

"No, no problem," father said as he sat down awkwardly on the floor.

"Well clearly, you're fired," Mr. Haggerty said. "Might as well get that out of the way right up top. And believe me, Watson, I don't get any pleasure in telling you that. This erection I have is a side effect of the blood pressure medication I've been taking and has nothing to do with me firing you."

He shifted in his chair and continued: "It's just that, even on your best day, you weren't very good at your job. Ambition. Teamwork. Results. These are the core values at Motherlove

Incorporated. The world is big, big place, and we're all just really small. Each one of us does our tiny part. If we can't join together and work towards the greater good, then what hope does the future hold?"

James said nothing.

22

Had my father been fired four years ago, when he was still attempting to build a life for himself and his ex-wife Petra, he might've coughed out a few pathetic *you-can't-do-this-to-mes* or *I-need-this-jobs*. He might've even tossed in a righteously indignant *oh-yeah?-well-you-can't-fire-me-because-I-quit!* before he stormed out the door. But the truth of the matter is, at this moment in time, after his fatal diagnosis and all the emotional bear traps therein, all he could feel was relief.

What is a rainstorm if you're already wet?

23

Of course, this was his life as he had lived it:

He had gotten hired at Motherlove Incorporated right out of high school. Right after he met Petra. Back when he figured all the pieces would somehow slide themselves comfortably into place.

Motherlove was the only job he ever had.

He was in the Paint Division. In quality control.

He'd show up in the morning, in his freshly ironed suit, and he'd sit at his little desk in his little cubicle, somewhere in that endless office floor, and turn on his computer screen. There were no programs on his computer. No Messenger or iTunes. No Google. No internet access at all. There wasn't even solitaire.

Instead, when he turned his computer on, there would only be the live video feed of a wall. It was a high-definition video, displayed with as many pixels as the current technology would allow. The wall would be freshly painted. Sometimes the paint was Celebration Blue© and sometimes it was Miami Green© and sometimes it was Apricots & Sugarcanes©. It was James's job to sit there and watch it dry, taking note of any irregularities and inconsistencies as the color settled.

That was it.

24

But back in Mr. Haggerty's office:

"Okay," was what James finally said, acknowledging his boss.

"Okay?" said Mr. Haggerty.

James shrugged. "Yeah. Okay. I guess I'm fired then."

"Yes, you are."

"And like I said, okay then."

There was a pregnant pause, swollen and obvious. Haggerty bit his lip and his nostrils flared further.

"So wait a second," he said. "You're not going to scream at me?"

"Wasn't planning on it, no," said James.

"You're not gonna to cry? Genuflect at my feet? Beg for mercy?"

"Nope."

"….but you're at least going to curse me out, right? C'mon. Call me a prick. Call me a fat asshole. Threaten to take a shit in the gas tank of my car."

"Would it make you feel better if I did?"

"I mean, a little bit, yeah."

"If you really want me to shit in your gas tank, I will."

"No, no, no," a distraught Mr. Haggerty said. "If your heart isn't it in, don't even bother."

"So…does that mean I can go now, or…?" James asked.

"Yeah. Yeah, you can go."

25

James Watson was sent to Human Resources to fill out his exit paperwork, sign legal documents that stated he accepted the terms his termination.

Under the section labeled 'reasons for leaving?' he sliced his palm open with a thumbtack and squeezed the blood out all over the paper. Under the section labeled 'what did you like most about your time working for Motherlove Incorporated?' he stuck a finger down his throat and forced himself to vomit up some whiskey-hot bile. The HR lady was not amused. She used the HR tongs to remove the moist sheet of paper from the countertop and stuff it into the filing cabinet behind her.

"Well, this is it. Guess I'll be seeing you around, Marcie," James said to her with a nod.

"My name is Janet," she replied as he walked away.

James was then sent to the office of Dr. Anne, the company's in-house psychologist.

As I alluded to in an earlier chapter, my father's relationship with Dr. Anne was soon to blossom into something much more substantial than that of your typical patient/practitioner. But before that:

It was Dr. Anne's job first to screen, and then to determine, if the newly-discharged employee was inclined to come back to the office with…oh, let's say an automatic rifle…and shoot up the place.

Before Motherlove Incorporated employed Dr. Anne, there was a mass shooting somewhere in the building at least once a week. With her influence, that number had dropped by nearly seven percent! She was very good at what she did.

Unlike Mr. Haggerty, she had a chair for James to sit on. A couch too, in case he was more comfortable laying down. It was a familiar scene, all told, not dissimilar to the office of Dr. Caterwaul, the man who had twice delivered to James Watson some unfortunate news.

"I don't like doctors," my father said to her.

Dr. Anne had put a clothespin on her nose so she wouldn't have to smell him.

"It's just a job," she said. "I hope you won't hold it against me."

"The thing is, I have this black spot in my brain," he said. "It's fatal. A doctor—a doctor like YOU—told me about it two weeks ago."

"That's unfortunate. On behalf of everyone in the entire

medical community, I want to offer you my condolences…"

"Thank yo—wait, is that sarcasm?"

"No," she said, and then, "Well, maybe it was. I'm not even sure anymore. It's not easy to give a shit, ya know? Everyone who comes in here has some kind of stupid problem and I'm supposed to just sit here and nod along like a bobblehead on the dashboard of a Subaru. I got my own shit I'm dealing with too, but it's always like, no, no, no, let's talk about YOU some more…"

James shifted uneasily in his seat, and continued:

"Well I—uh—I tried to give myself a lobotomy."

"Oh?"

"Yeah. To get the black spot out. It didn't work, obviously. I don't know how to perform brain surgery. I don't even know how to do basic math. I barely graduated high school. But is that so wrong? Is it wrong that I never knew what I wanted to *do* with my life? Like I was supposed to just make up my mind one day and then everything else would fall into place. I was just a kid back then. Shit, doc, I still feel like a kid. A dying kid.

"And the worst part is, if I had the chance to do it all over again, I know it'd play out in the same exact way. How could I even avoid it? It feels like fate, but not magical like that. It's more like…biology. It's like, a fundamental part of who I am. It's my personality. It's this damn black spot. IT'S ME.

"Plus, even if I *did* know what I wanted out of life, what difference would that make? Knowing what you want doesn't automatically make it obtainable. I was just never any good at taking tests. I was a straight D student then. I am a straight D human being now."

"Life can sometimes feel like a series of tests, can't it?" she said.

"I guess," he said. "Though I feel like you're just agreeing with me because you're a psychologist and that's what you're supposed to do…"

"Yes, I can see how you might feel that way."

"You're doing it right now!"

"I am, aren't I?"

"Look lady, I don't need to be pandered to. I can see that clothespin on your nose. I smell horrible and we both know it! There's no reason for either of us to pretend otherwise."

"Sure, I have a clothespin on my nose, but to be fair, you smell *exceptionally* bad. Like, you walked in here and my first instinct was to chop my nose clean off my face so I wouldn't have to encounter anything so horrible ever again. But I didn't do that, did I Mr. Watson? I didn't chop my nose off, which I easily could've done, because I keep a knife nearby, just in case it were to ever come to that."

She slowly pulled a serrated 10-inch tactical knife out from under the cushion of her chair and held it up for James Watson to inspect. There was a rusty smear of brown along the curve of the blade. Dried blood.

"How about I make a deal with you?" she said.

"What's that?"

"Instead of me blindly agreeing with you, I'll stab you in the neck if you say something I don't like. That way, you'll know that I'm actually listening."

She placed the knife on her lap. The steel against her bare legs, right where her skirt ended.

"Now, please continue, Mr. Watson…"

27

So James continued:

"You know the only reason I kept working here as long as I did was because of Petra. Petra still worked here, and so, I still worked here too."

"Petra is…?"

"My wife. My *ex*-wife, I should say. She left me when she found out I couldn't have children…"

He sighed heavily and glared at Dr. Anne.

"That's what you doctors do, ya know," he said. "Y'all act like you answer to this higher calling, bound, you claim, by the Hippocratic Oath or whatever the fuck it's called. You swear to us regular folks that you'll do no harm. But, in truth, you're thieves."

"Thieves?" she said. "I'm afraid I'm not following…"

She held up the knife and threateningly pointed it at him.

"Thieves of hope," he clarified. "People wanna act like despair is the opposite of hope, but really, the opposite of hope is *truth*. You can grapple with despair, and you can pull yourself out of it. It's conquerable. But you can't argue with the truth."

"Mr. Watson, you'd still have the same fatal disease, even if there wasn't a doctor around to diagnose it."

"Yeah, but I wouldn't KNOW about it."

"That's not a cure."

"It's not the black spot that's gonna kill me, doctor. It's *knowing* there's a black spot there. It's having to look the darkness in the face, every goddamn day, and remind myself that death is not some intangible thing that's only reserved for other people. It's mine, to carry, to hold, a part of me. How am I supposed to go on? How am I supposed to function? How do I reconcile the knowledge that the world will be spinning whether I'm here or not? How can I accept that the world has always spun, will continue to spin?"

My father was in full-on hysterics now. He had slid off his chair and was rolling around on the floor. Fat tears ran from his clenched eyes like the juice from pressed grapes. His dick flopped out of his boxer shorts and lay, unshaved and shriveled, against his leg. There was a grease stain left on the carpet where his body had touched it.

It was, quite honestly, the most pathetic thing Dr. Anne had ever seen.

"Just stab me already," he wailed. "Get it over with. Cut my fucking head off!"

[Spoiler alert: Dr. Anne doesn't stab James Watson right here in her office. That scene will come later, in a couple of more chapters, in James Watson's kitchen in the house that he and Petra used to share.]

Instead, Dr. Anne continued her psychological assessment by pulling out a series of Rorschach test cards from a desk drawer. Symmetrical inkblots splayed against backgrounds of white. My father was still rolling about on the floor like a buffoon when she held up the first card.

"Tell me, Mr. Watson, what do you see?"

"Are you fucking with me, doc? That's a picture of the black spot inside of my head, hemorrhaging across the page!"

"And this one?"

"That is what I will see on my deathbed as my life flashes before my eyes."

"And this?"

"That one is an abstract artist's interpretation of the sound of my voice when I tell you I'm fucking dying over here!"

She put the cards down.

"Alright, so let's just say, for the sake of argument, that you weren't dying…"

"Huh?" he said.

"It's a little thought experiment. Humor me for a second," she said. "Let's say you weren't dying anymore. Let's say the sky opened up and God leaned down from the clouds to answer your prayers, face to face. He's the benevolent God of storybooks, He cares about you. He's God with a capital G. Let's say He decided to grant you a stay of execution. What would you do with your newfound time?"

James stopped writhing, though his nose still ran and his eyes still pickled in his sockets. He tucked his genitals back into his shorts and took a deep breath. His dolphin-soft chest rose and fell as he considered what the doctor had just said to him.

"What would I do?"

"What would you do?"

"I—I don't know..."

"Perhaps that's the question you should be asking yourself," she said.

James climbed to his feet. His face flummoxed.

"I'm not quite sure where I would even begin..."

"You can begin by leaving my office and carrying on with the rest of your day," she said.

"The rest of my day?"

"Today first. Then tomorrow. Then the next day. And then the day after that."

28

But before my father left her office, as she had just instructed of him, the good doctor did something she's usually not inclined to do.

Several months later, after a night of passionate lovemaking with the now-very-pregnant-with-me James Watson, Dr. Anne recounted the moment the two of them met in her Motherlove office, and she spoke of the thought processes that were going through her brain.

"I've always believed in true love," she shamefully confessed, her breath just a whisper, her bare arm draped affectionately across my father's swollen stomach. "It's illogical, I know, but sometimes the world needs to be given a shape regardless."

She said: "All human beings are deep wells of contradictory emotions."

She said: "Our motivations are as nebulous as they are varied."

She said: "This drive I have is insatiable. And it makes no sense. It's as much a part of me as my fingers are. You came to me, James, so pitiful and sick. A hopeless case, if I ever saw one. But when I looked at you, I didn't see a broken man; I saw a newborn infant."

She said: "If I can fix just one person, perhaps I could somehow fix myself."

She said these things knowing they were (metaphorically-speaking) her black spot to bear.

But she was right. The world was shapeless. And most people don't even care. As fruitless as it may be, she wanted to help.

So perhaps that was the reason why, on the day my father

got fired from Motherlove Incorporated, when he got up and went to leave her office, Dr. Anne reached out her hand and said, "Wait."

And he stood there, one foot in the room and the other foot in the hall, as she handed him her business card, upon which she had scribbled her personal cellphone number.

"Look, life is hard, James, I'm well aware of that. But...you can call me if you need me."

My father slid the card in his pocket and said:

"You know I'm not going to come back and shoot up the place, right?"

"Well I'm certainly glad to hear that," the doctor replied.

But on the form she had to fill out after he left, under the line labeled DOES THE FORMER EMPLOYEE POSE A THREAT TO THE SAFETY AND WELLBEING OF THE REST OF THE COMPANY? Dr. Anne checked the tiny box labeled 'maybe.'

29

Many, many years later:

A small commercial fishing vessel recovered my father's dead body from the Indian Ocean. He floated face down on the surface, his skin like a tarpaulin, wide and thin and flat, stretching for miles. He certainly didn't look remotely human anymore.

They pulled him aboard and folded him up like a newspaper and shipped him back to the city in a plastic crate. On the outside of the crate was a sticker that read BIOHAZARD.

There was the question of what we should do with his remains. Some said we should cremate him. Others wanted to tether him to weights and drop him back into the sea. The then-mayor, Isabel Gaynor, proposed we have him stuffed and mounted above City Hall.

"He could be like our mascot," she said.

But I pooh-poohed that quick.

"I think we should build him a tomb," I said. "We should erect a massive tomb. Like a pyramid, or an obelisk. Something big and ugly and unavoidable, like the man himself. And then we bury him beneath it, and write HERE LIES JAMES WATSON, THE FATHER OF ALL MANKIND on the top, and we surround it with cerulean fountains and arched trestles of lilac, oak, and wisteria."

"Bury him?" Mayor Gaynor said.

"Like a seed," I replied.

I wanted to put his body in place where the public could

come and reflect. Calm and quiet, like a Japanese garden. I wanted it so you could walk along a beautiful pathway, or sit on one of the natural benches, and meditate on your formerly fragile mortality. You beautiful immortal bastard, did you remember when the human race had once gone mad in the face of the yawning abyss? Did you realize how lucky you were that that abyss had finally been bridged? Here you were on the other side, triumphant. The future was limitless. Death had been cured.

The Motherlove marketing department called it Infinitassium. It was a once-daily supplement. You took it with your morning coffee. It regenerated cells, flushed your body of unwanted pathogens, preserved cognitive ability, and halted (and in some cases reversed) the aging process. Barring accidents, homicide, suicide, and other unforeseen calamities, it would essentially let the consumer live forever.

I invented Infinitassium using my father's cloning formula and my own DNA.

The Death of Death was what the article written about me in *Time* was titled.

Mortal No More was the one that appeared in the *New Yorker,* alongside a picture of me in a lab coat holding a beaker of greenish liquid. Both the coat and beaker were props. I didn't actually do any real science. I didn't really do anything, besides showing up with a few fresh ideas. I was more like…a loose key that happened to find the right lock.

Regardless, Mayor Gaynor agreed with my proposal and some of the monthly budget was allocated towards the construction of The James Watson Memorial Garden. A crew was hired; architects and stonecutters and landscapers and custodians. A large granite structure was erected in the westernmost corner of Elysium Grounds, the fancy cemetery in the city's poshest neighborhood. Interred in that very same dirt were the most influential people from around town. A couple of congressmen. A few business magnates. The movers and shakers. A movie star or two.

The monolith towered above the other nearby headstones. It cast shadows across the rest of the graveyard. Beneath the soil he lay, the final fatality, the last human being to ever die, and rot.

On the side of the monolith was a plaque. On it was a cryptic aphorism that read:

FIRST
THERE IS A MOUNTAIN
THEN
THERE IS NO MOUNTAIN
THEN
THERE IS

30

Everything I mentioned in that last chapter happened, more or less, in the terrifyingly brief but beautiful moment before The Gray Tide came crashing down upon our shores.

"What is The Gray Tide?" you ask.

It is the apocalypse I accidently helped to engineer.

It is how you died.

It is how I ended the world.

Regular folks used to be buried at Park West Memorial, on the opposite side of the city, as far away from Elysium Grounds as you could possibly get. If they were still burying people, then Park West is where my final resting place would be, under a potter's field, amid a sea of weather-stripped headstones, unmarked and unknown, a slightly discolored patch of grass the only proof I was ever here at all.

But no such tribunal formed. There was no one left to make me atone for my sins, to pay for my hubris. There is no punishment coming my way, save The Tide itself, and that same punishment came for us all, regardless of what we had done.

The Gray Tide holds no judgment. That much is clear. And even if it did, it would undoubtedly thank me for my part in its creation. It would call me brother. Call me kin. Give me a big, familial hug as it melted me away in its hungry, inescapable grasp.

The last news report we received said The Tide has spread as far west as Australia, chewing away at the edges of the island-continent like rust on a tin can, like a fungus on a tree stump, until the landmass broke apart and sank in the writing foam.

Then the television and internet went out.

Motherlove Incorporated still continued to turn a profit, of course, even in the darkness, even though all of the people who used to benefit from that profit are either unaccounted for or dead. Everyone is either unaccounted for or dead. Everyone, that is, except for me and a handful of my closest subordinates who had nowhere else to go. We have been hiding out in The Impossible Room in the now-abandoned Motherlove Building downtown, waiting for the end ourselves. All the money in the world apparently wasn't enough to save the bigwigs and CEOs at Motherlove. When The Tide finally reached the city's shores, they all went home to be with their families. But I came here. I too had nowhere else to go.

The Gray Tide crept out of the Indian Ocean, marching forward like a primordial army, and the stock market kept on ticking by, completely automated, without the need for a single human being to catalog those numbers or care. But, GODDAMN IT, I still care. Someone has to! Someone has to run the company. Someone has to survive this thing. Someone has to pass this story along. Someone has to write this book. Someone has to benefit from all the generations that have come and gone, to reap the fruit of this amassed knowledge, this consolidated effort, this pain and fear and grief and misery. It can't all be for nothing, can it? Something is going to happen to save us. Or to give this all meaning. This isn't *actually* the end of the world, right? Right?!??

I had only wanted to help people. To help myself. To live forever.

This is all my fault, isn't it?

I am the black spot upon the Planet Earth.

31

But let's talk more about the day that James Watson was fired from Motherlove Incorporated, and all the strange and coincidental things that happened thereafter:

You see, there was no bus that ran from downtown to Sycamore Lane in the middle of the day, so my father had to call for a taxi to drive him home.

In the backseat of the cab James Watson's bare belly rested on top of his knees as he told the driver about his terminal illness and how Dr. Anne granted him a stay of execution.

"She just said the word. She said the word 'live' and suddenly, I was reborn. I was alive."

"Just one word?" said the cab driver.

"That's all it took."

"That's not much."

"No, that's not much at all."

"Then today is a miracle, is it not, yes?"

"A small miracle," my father agreed, "It sure is."

"Seems to me that god must have some tiny hands," the cabbie said, the eyes of the two men meeting in the rearview mirror. "He only works in miracles so small some might say they don't even exist."

32

Of course, Dr. Anne's offhanded suggestion that my father go out and *"seize the day"* didn't function as the cure-all he immediately proclaimed it to be. That wasn't how it worked. You couldn't swallow advice like an Infinitassium tablet and expect to be a different person when the next sun rises. Fixing a leak takes way more effort than making a hole.

So even though he was feeling slightly more in control, he wasn't quite absolved of all the guilt, anger, and trepidation by which he had been previously consumed. He was still a man very much in the throes of an existential breakdown, and The Reaper loomed nearer still, as dark as the mud that filled up his skull. But the good doctor's words affected him nonetheless, like aloe rubbed onto a burn, and he was slowly able to get a grip, at least enough to stop screaming every time he saw his own reflection.

Opening the front door to the marital home he and Petra once shared, James Watson was again greeted by the frightful mess he had left behind.

"What have I done?" he said mournfully to himself, walking slowly from room to room.

And so he tried to fix it. He tried to clean up his kitchen.

He got down on his hands and knees and used bleach and soap and water to get the splattered condiments out of all the cracks in the tile floor. This proved to be impossible, of course. The roaches and the fungus watched from the wings of the room, until he gave up.

"Good enough," he said to himself, and, for the moment, it was.

33

Unfortunately for James though, death was not something that could be easily circumnavigated with a positive attitude and a little bit of elbow grease. You can't bleach away your pain. You can't pour turpentine on the human heart. People live their whole lives trying to avoid this fact, carting their hearts around like cast-iron anchors. Ribcages like prisons, like zoo bars for elephants; here we are, shackled to our own despair, and misery was a trough so deep that everyone could have their fill. Look around and you'll find hearts that were like the kitchen floor of my father's house, caked up with mayonnaise and mildew and rot. You'll find hearts of former lovers that had grown stagnant and cold over time. You'll find hearts that were once gorged with passion which now thumped only for themselves. You'll find hearts that were broken. Hearts now unsalvageable.

So does any of this make James Watson special? No, no, no, not at all. We should not laud him for refusing to bury his sadness under the porch. This was a morbid and pathetic display. A well-adjusted person would not spread their sadness around like it was Thanksgiving dinner, then force everyone around them to eat it, including me, after I was cloned from his cells, and born. I am a product of both nature and nurture, two horrible coconspirators, relentlessly plotting against me. All of this to simply say:

My father had cleaned up his kitchen, but his house was still a mess.

34

And yet here he was, in the bedroom, collecting up all his shoes and shirts and pants.

Here he was pushing his mattress down the stairs, letting it tumble forward, end over end.

Here he was, awkwardly dragging his sofa out the door, chopping up his coffee table and carrying out the splinters, emptying out the bathroom, purging the garage.

He worked the entire rest of the day, until all his possessions, everything he had ever owned, was stacked up in the front yard in a pile that stood taller than he did.

Then he set the entire thing on fire.

35

Flames licked at the leaves of the trees. Black smoke filled the sky. If Hell were confined to such a limited space, then his front yard surely would be the devil's playground.

The fire was raging when the bus from the Motherlove Building downtown finally rolled up to the local stop, around 6 o'clock that evening.

Brad and Jennifer Flatly, Harrison and Tabitha Moss, and all the other husbands and wives of Sycamore Lane stepped off, in single-file, but instead of immediately retreating to the aluminum-sided security of their respective homes, the neighbors all stood in stark silence and watched as James Watson's pyre grew bigger. My mostly-naked father danced in front of it like the wind around a volcano.

Eventually though, everyone grew bored of this grotesque display, and they all left to go eat their dinners and watch their televisions and sleep in their beds and do it all again tomorrow.

Brad Flatly was the only one to come over. He slowly walked across the grass and then laid a hand on James Watson's sweat-covered back. James stopped bopping around and turned around to face him.

"So—um—you doin' okay, buddy?" Brad asked.

"Me? Never better," my father replied, his voice no more affected than if they had just run into each other at the bank.

"I heard that Haggerty gave you the boot earlier. No ceremony or nothing. Just 'get your shit and get out.' Wham-bam-thank you, ma'am. How about that, after what—15 years of loyal service?"

James absently nodded as the fire crackled and flared up higher.

"Rumor is that you took it like a champ, though. They say you didn't scream or cry or take a crap in your hand and smear it all over the walls or nothing! Still, that's gotta be tough news to process, on top of finding out about the brain tumor and all…"

"It's a black spot, not a tumor," James said.

"What's the difference?" Brad asked.

James just shrugged. "I don't know."

"Well whatever it is, that's some rotten luck you got. Not that I didn't see the axe headed your way. We all knew it was gonna happen, we'd been talking about it for weeks. And shit, I'da gone to bat for you too, buddy, but you know how it is, office politics being what they are. I gotta cover my own ass first or I'mma end up in the breadline right next to you. And if Jennifer left me like Petra left you—jeez, I don't know WHAT I'd do. Probably shoot up the place. Ha ha ha. I will say, though, that you were one of the best paint-watchers I've ever met. In fact, when I was in college--"

"It's beautiful, isn't it?" my father interrupted his neighbor as he motioned towards the burning heap.

"Huh?"

"The fire. It's beautiful, yes?" my father repeated himself. A lawnmower in the pile started to burn.

"I mean, it's certainly hot…"

"You know, if you wanted, you could throw all your stuff into the pile too, Brad…"

As James said these words, he held onto his neighbor by the shoulders. Brad tried to wiggle free, but when he realized how tight my father's grip was, he stopped and instead offered to James a weak but conciliatory smile.

"James, you're—you're hurting me…" he said through gritted teeth.

"We can burn this entire cul-de-sac to the ground," my

father said, his eyes opening, wide and wild. "We can start over. We can rebuild it, out of the ashes. Build it better. Do it right next time…"

Brad didn't know how to respond. And honestly, what could he have said anyway?

The fire's saffron light crashed into the maroon of the setting sun and long shadows found their way into the contours of James's face. It made him look terrifyingly intense. Brad took in the man next to him and felt a wave of fear, like he was in the presence of a monster. Luckily for him (and for you too, fair reader, if you, like Brad Flatly, were finding this scene a bit too intense) neither of you were left to be scared for very long. For the gas tank on the burning lawnmower had ignited and exploded. With a cacophonous *Ka-BOOM* it sent flaming shrapnel out in all directions at once. Most of it was harmless: now-crispy couch stuffing and old pages of newspaper, both rendered to ash before hitting the ground. This explosion barely warranted mentioning, save for a single projectile, which found itself an unlikely target.

It was a screwdriver. A screwdriver on fire. It shot out of the burning garbage pile and flew through the air with the force of a bullet before it connected with my father's forehead.

It easily pierced his skull. It plunged into the soft meat that he housed in his cranium; stabbed him right in through the brain.

James Watson collapsed, motionless, onto the ground.

36

James Watson lay there, injured and unconscious, but he was not dead. And the scene that had just unfolded in my father's front yard was not nearly as gory as you would've expected. If you leaned in and looked closely, you could plainly see that there was hardly any blood leaking from the wound at all. That is because the impact and angle of the screwdriver didn't fragment my father's skull. It didn't explode open the side of his head like he had swallowed a stick of TNT. The tip of the tool entered his brain like a sniper's bullet, cleanly, nestling itself between the already well-trod ridges of his prefrontal cortex before poking, ever-so-slightly, into his amygdala. It lodged itself in there, in just the right place, so as to not be fatal; one of those situations where if it had landed a millimeter more in any direction, he would've surely suffered irreparable damage.

And so, he woke up hours later, further broken but still alive, the only lasting effects being that his eyes were no longer able to blink in unison and there was the unsightly plastic handle of a cheap K-Mart screwdriver poking out of the center of his forehead like a half-melted unicorn horn.

37

He slowly climbed to his feet. Aside from the frame of the house itself, everything he had ever owned had been consumed by fire, rendered into a snowdrift of smoldering ash in the yard. It was nighttime and the only sound he heard was crickets and the air passing in and out of his lungs.

His balance was unreliable. He teetered on weak knees, seasick.

He wondered, for a moment, if the Earth was quaking beneath him, though he knew that was probably not the case. The ground was as immovable as it ever was, and after only a few steps he had learned to properly walk once again. A few more steps after that and he could've even danced if he wanted to, which he most certainly did not.

He made his way back inside, not bothering to close the front door behind him, stumbling around in the dark, now-lampless living room. There was nothing to bang his knees against, no end tables or ottomans to impede his path, but he wove around like they were there anyway, navigating their ghosts.

He found the bathroom, flicked on the switch and turned on the sink in one single motion, scooping handfuls of rusty water into his dry mouth. In that moment, my father was a thirsty man! It wasn't until he finished drinking that he finally looked up into the mirror and saw the screwdriver sticking out of his head.

"Oh shit."

He touched it and pain like lightning spread across his face. His teeth clenched so hard they almost shattered to pieces. Removing the tool didn't seem to be an option. He imagined pulling it out would've caused his brain to squirt out of the hole, like a popped pimple, like pulling the cork out of a barrel of merlot.

He did lean in and inspect it closer though. His skin already seemed to be healing around the handle. It was like it didn't want to let the screwdriver go.

"How am I alive?" he said out loud, to no one.

"I know it seems unlikely, but there is a reason for this," I answer him now, across the reaches of both time and space. "There is a reason for everything, dad. That's how science works!"

Of course, I say that like it were so simple, like I'm about to explain everything to you now, but the truth is, even I don't know what that reason is. I, like my father before me, don't understand the first fucking thing about science, even though, by title and trade, I am technically a scientist. Dr. Jimmy Watson Jr. I was called, the once-head of Research and Development for Motherlove Incorporated.

But scientific explanations be damned, you can't deny a coincidence when it's right there sticking out of your head. And coincidences will come to pass, with or without reason, with or without explanation, with or without empirical proof. Unlike biology, genetics, math, and chemistry, coincidences are conceptually simple and absolute, and here's an example to illustrate my point:

Let's say some highly improbable thing just occurred. Let's say—oh I dunno—a terminally-ill man survived a should-be-fatal stab wound to the noggin and then decided to impregnate himself with his own clone. People will look at this event, and all the events that led up to it and all the events that it inspired, and say to themselves "Gee, I wonder what the chances of that are?" and I will be right there behind them to reply with great confidence: "Well, if it's already happened, there's no need to wonder at all, because those chances were clearly 100%!"

38

So a screwdriver entered my father's skull at such a speed and angle that not only did it lodge itself between the rucks of his brain like an Arthurian sword, but the elusive and malignant black spot that had been creeping around the inside of his head didn't have a chance to duck out of its way either. It was slithering around in his thoughts like a malicious slug, totally oblivious to the happenings of the outside world. And when the stainless steel projectile poked its way through my father's forehead, it also poked its way through the globby rotten center of the black spot, too. It pinned that quivering ebony mass in place, pressing it tight against his frontal lobe.

At first, the black spot raged. It thrashed and belted. It dug its liquid claws into the folds in my father's brain and attempted to tear its way out of his head. It certainly didn't like being trapped, and as it fought against its newfound captivity, it jumbled up James Watson's thoughts like a highway accident. The distinctions that normally separated events, the causes and effects, the pasts and the futures, all blended into a singular, indistinguishable whole. It was a moment of pure confusion. Of mental disassociation. Of ego death:

There is no such thing as James Watson. I am a creature of pure thought. I am an eternal reflection, a refraction, a repurposing of energy, in a constant cycle of birth and death.

Stuff like that.

And in that jumble, out of time, he even saw the end of

this book. He knows where this and all his decisions will lead. And he knows he will follow them just as they are written here. You too could simulate this experience, see the world as James Watson did then, by skipping ahead and reading the last paragraph before continuing on. The words on these pages won't shift places while you're gone. You have the ability to read them in any order you please.

The point is, there was no James Watson anymore, not in the cognitive sense, in the bathroom in the house at the end of Sycamore Lane. He was just a corporeal shell, hanging above this hissing sink like an empty hazmat suit.

But that moment eventually passed, as they all do. The clock kept ticking. The black spot settled into place, immobile as it now was. Time laid back down, nice and linear. And as James Watson was once again able to regulate his breathing and lower his heartbeat, he blinked, his eyelids slightly out-of-sync, and saw his face reform in the mirror, one atom at a time.

39

For James Watson, whose brain was now blessed with a screwdriver through the center of it, all of these conflicting thoughts and emotions culminated in formation of an idea.

It came to him in a flash, in much the way he always imagined novelists got inspired. Like an egg-timer goes off, like *BING!* and there it is. An idea, fresh out of the oven, perfectly cooked.

PLEASE NOTE THOUGH: that as someone who is LITERALLY in the middle of writing the novel you are currently reading, I can assure you that god does not dole out genius like some sort of drunken Santa Claus. Not one of the words I have written so far has come to me on a silver platter. I have struggled with every sentence. I do not have a screwdriver in my head like my father did. The most ironic part of all this is, of course, that I am writing this book for no one. The rest of the world is already dead. They've been washed away in The Gray Tide. And even if someone out there somehow managed to survive thus far, it won't be for much longer anyway. It's inevitable. So I tell you now while I still can: at best inspiration is a tempest that builds in the darkness before being carried to fruition, if it is lucky enough to be carried to fruition at all. No matter how much ink is spilled, there will always remain more to be said.

Under any other circumstances, a moment like this would've surely felt scary, or overwhelming, or soul-crushingly intense, or any number of other uncontrollable emotions. Some may have called it madness. Some may have even called

James Watson a mad scientist, as the idea that just appeared in his head is not that of a person thinking rationally.

But my father, James Watson, was not a man of science. He was a desperate, ephemeral fool on the precipice of an impossible oblivion, grasping for something—ANYTHING—to call his own.

And then he found it:

He was going to unravel the mysteries of the human genome.

He was going to clone himself.

And he was going impregnate himself with that clone.

He was going to have a son.

"Don't scoff!" I say to you now. "It's true! It's true!"

"C'mon, that's ridiculous," you say. "It doesn't make any sense. How do you expect us not to laugh? And even so, were we to foolishly accept such a concept at face value, what are the odds of it even working in the first place?"

Well…as I am the end product of that very idea, I can conclusively tell you with great confidence: "The odds of it working were 100%!"

PART TWO:
GESTATION

40

So I bet you're wondering how my father came up with his cloning formula.

It's a valid concern. It's the crux of this entire story. It's important.

Later, I will take that very same formula to Motherlove myself, and they will use it to develop Infinitassium, and cure death.

On a scientific and logistical level, all of this seems neigh impossible. How? How? How?

Well, to answer your question as bluntly as possible: I don't exactly know how!

Even working with his formula, as I have done for nearly a decade, parlaying that into a successful career for myself here at Motherlove Incorporated, I still don't know!

I imagine he had to go out to the store, since he didn't own any possessions anymore, and pick himself up a chemistry kit. Probably a microscope or something like that. A pen and paper. Some surgical supplies. Maybe a few books like *What to Expect When You're Expecting?* or *Dr. Spock's Baby and Child Care.* Maybe he rented *Junior,* that 1994 Arnold Schwarzenegger comedy wherein he impregnates himself and then falls in love with Emma Thompson. I think Danny DeVito was in that movie too, I don't know, it's been awhile since I've seen it.

Then I suspect my father brought all his new toys down into his basement, where the sun/moon cycle above would not be able disturb his thoughts. For him, the basement could seem like an endless day, a place with no clocks to *tick tick tick* and remind him that the hour had changed.

And then he tinkered, hypothesized, experimented. It was a lengthy process of trial and error, I'm sure, because the truth was he didn't know what he was doing either. He was in uncharted biological territory. He was alit on a sea of flesh and fluids. He was bobbing for molecules.

In the end he managed to locate some particularly responsive cells on his body. Then he cut those cells loose, cut them into pieces, smaller and smaller, until he was picking out the strands of DNA like confetti off the floor after a New Year's Eve party. He poked and prodded that confetti using needles and knifes. He turned the sludge into serums, turned the serums into vapors, turned the vapors into crystals, turned the crystals back into sludge to begin the process anew.

And if things started to change, it was imperceptible at first, and time passed by like the invisible borders that separated two countries: First he was in Spain, then he was in France.

In retrospect, his progress was obvious. I am telling you now it eventually worked. But in the moment, as it unfolded, it felt like chaos. James Watson was in turmoil, but his focus never wavered.

It was the screwdriver in his skull that was steering him along, of course, stimulating and stirring those previously unused areas of his brain. You could throw a millions screwdrivers into a million bonfires and never replicate these particular results. It is why I—in my official capacity as Motherlove Incorporated's Chief Technician of Research and Development—had instructed my team to jam various sharp objects into their heads, in varying angles. One fellow even dug a butter knife in the space between his eyeball and bottom eyelid and wiggled it around for a while, left and right, up and down, hoping to get that flash of genius. Still, nothing.

Anyway, James Watson mixed a whole bunch of random chemicals and cells together. The technical details don't matter. He might as well have flapped his arms around and he quoted Shakespeare like "*Double double toil and trouble, fire burn and cauldron bubble...*" because it must've felt like witch's magic when, suddenly, there I was, a microscopic zygote, a perfect copy of his genetic code, twitching around in a jelly-filled petri dish.

Welcome to France!

41

When I was 11, my father had "the talk" with me.

We discussed the birds and the bees, where babies come from, and he attempted to teach me the secrets of his cloning technique.

"Why would a bird have sex with a bee?" he said. Already, his body was ten times the size he was when I was just a baby, taking up a good portion of the basement and more. He had been growing. He was barely able to move, his torso gone wider in every direction, stomach flesh drooping down past his knees, unrolling like a wrestling mat. He didn't go upstairs much anymore, instead taking his meals in the corner of the basement, which served as his bedroom, bathroom, kitchen, and workspace.

There was the patter of tiny feet upstairs—a few dozen of my younger brothers—running all around the house. Since my conception, James Watson has been doubling and tripling up on the babies. Filling himself up with life, sticking them in every nook and cranny, before birthing them all out again. He was swelled up with them right then, three more fetuses, one in the front, one in the back, and the third incubated in a gland between his armpit and rib.

This is why his body was so big, stretched out to accommodate his temporary guests.

"Why isn't it the bees and the bees?" he continued. "A queen bee, and all her drones, nearly identical, a hive, an army entirely of one mindset, one purpose, one goal. Buzz buzz buzz, my children. We still have so much work to do!"

He tried to explain which particular substances he had used

to make me [serophene, letrozole, Windex, yogurt, menotropin] and in what quantities; how long he let that concoction sit, festering under the grow lamp in his dank basement. He told me where and how he inserted my fetus into his body, where I was stored for the next nine months of my development, before I was born back into the world.

"There were a lot of mistakes along the way," he said to me with a paternal chuckle. "A lot of missteps. But I'm getting better at it. I'm refining the process, even now. I've got the gestation period down to only 5 months, on the verge of breaking 4. After that 3. And then 2. Soon I'll figure out how to incubate another fetus under my skin, then another, then another. Maybe stack 'em up and get 'em smaller? Mr. Peapod, that's what they can call me. A James Watson factory, that's what I'll be. Now let me tell you about how to get the process started…"

At 11, I could only bite my tongue and embarrassedly listen on as my father told me about all the beakers and flasks he had masturbated into.

42

At present:

We've been holed up in the Motherlove Incorporated building for the last few days as the situation outside continued to deteriorate. It has not been easy. The Impossible Room, with its boundless walls, is where I've written the entirety of this manuscript so far. It's where I'm most likely going to die. No monuments will be erected when The Gray Tide finally reaches our door.

The lights are low in here. Air comes through the ventilation system in clunky spurts. Computers flicker on and off intermittently. We're on backup power. Whatever is left of the world is on backup power.

"Well the good news is that market shares are still up, my liege," Kelsey said to me with a submissive bow after checking the stock ticker on a nearby terminal.

"Thank you, Kels," I said. "That means we're on track to finish up 8% this quarter, which is good news for our stockholders, whom are all dead, which means by default I own the majority shares. Great job to you all, my loyal subjects!"

Oh, did I mention that I've declared myself the King of Motherlove Incorporated? Because as of last night, I'm the King of Motherlove now. Not that there was much debate or contention in that matter. *Someone* had to be in charge, right? And it certainly wasn't going to be Kelsey.

King Jimmy, I've been having them call me, and we're all trapped in here like bees. Buzz buzz buzz.

There are only three other survivors, besides myself.

There's Kelsey, my muffin-faced assistant, with his licorice-black hair and his insect-wide eyes and his crooked teeth and his crooked nose, cocked to the left, like it were begging you to hang your coat up on it.

Then there's Carol, who always wore shoes the same color as her lipstick, and who used to drink ginger tea every day before all the ginger tea ran out. She works in accounting. She keeps the books.

And, of course, there's Helen. My wife. The queen.

We are all that's left. We are humanity's last hope.

43

I am not a usurper. Just wanted to state that for the record. I did not take my throne by force.

There was no coup. No election. No campaign. No promotion. Just a vacancy, a vacuum, a void that needed filling, and I was simply the next in line in a long and vertical chain of command. Before me went the President, then the Vice-President, then all the CEOs and CFOs and COOs and the rest, then the entire Board of Directors in one fell swoop, the financers, the lawyers, and finally the department heads: Marketing, Human Resources, Logistics, and Tech. They are all long gone.

So I have accepted my role as King without much pomp or pageantry. On my Coronation Day we feasted on a bag of Doritos that we purloined from a vending machine and drank from a bottle of cheap whiskey found in a desk in one of the cubicles. It seemed like every other desk in this office had a liquor bottle stashed away in its bottom drawer.

Fuck it. I'm going to get drunk right now! What does it even matter? I can still tell you this story when I'm drunk. It's the only story left to tell. The last story. My story. I know it by heart.

Aside from the four of us wandering through the endless wastelands of Motherlove Incorporated's downtown HQ, I know of no other survivors, inside this building or out. I keep checking Facebook whenever the signal cuts back in, but I'm the only one still updating my status.

"It's the end of the world as we know it…AND I FEEL FINE!" I posted. A bit of gallows humor, I know, but it usually plays. And yet: ZERO LIKES!

"Where will we go?" my bride, Queen Helen, asked me last night.

"I don't know," I told her, trying my hardest not to break down into tears.

And still, we trudged on. Through the rows of desks and chairs stretched to the horizon line and beyond, stopping to sleep when we got tired, stopping to eat when we got hungry, shitting and pissing wherever we damn well pleased. And yet, where are we truly headed? How long do we really have? What is the point of any of this? The Impossible Room might be infinitely big, but against The Gray Tide is infinity big enough?

The planet has surely slipped off its axis by now, though there's no news outlets to report on such an event. But I know how it would've gone. The Gray Tide would've eaten up half the Earth without a second thought. That's what The Gray Tide does. It eats and eats. It would've chewed through the crust, chewed though the mantle, chewed its way down to the planet's molten core and then chewed that up too. If you were on the moon looking down at us right now, it would look like a massive space dragon had stopped by to have a snack, taken a giant bite out of the planet before moving on. This Cookie Earth. But death did not come above. It came from inside. It came from inside my father. Inside of ME.

Now we're careening out of orbit, spinning sideways, falling away from the sun into icy space. The Gray Tide on the ground, and now, gray clouds above, gray snow whipping in between, like a fog. Gray everything. Gray Death.

44

We had stopped to camp for the night. Kelsey set a copy machine on fire. We huddled around it, keeping warm.

I think: one of these cubicles must've belonged to my father, James Watson. He spent good portion of his life here, watching paint dry.

I think: how differently would things have turned out if just one variable had been tweaked, if Petra had never left him, if he could've had children the traditional way, if one chink in his crooked chain had been corrected.

I think: when he worked here, I wasn't yet a person. I wasn't even a thought in his head. I would come charging in later, on a flaming screwdriver, ready to tear his old life to shreds, as unstoppable as The Tide he and I created. How could James Watson have known, during the long and lugubrious years he spent in this building, that he would one day sire a king?

If I opened a window, I'd be able to hear his voice trapped in The Gray Tide, screaming.

But I don't ask him questions because I know he won't answer.

45

And then suddenly, as I composed these words, there was this:

Just outside our bubble of fire light, a clatter. A rustle and smash. Old paper reports crunched under moving feet. We all whipped our heads in its direction. From the darkness, more shuffling.

There was someone, some*thing*, out there, and it was approaching us quickly.

I held up a stapler, ready to protect my kingdom, whatever the cost.

"Who goes there?" I shouted. "Show yourself or so help me god, I will staple your t-shirt to your chest and it will be very uncomfortable for you!"

"Don't shoot," a voice wavered as an older, white-haired gentleman stepped out of the shadows. His wrinkled face was covered with deep tan lines, the way the topography of Utah might look if viewed from a plane, and skinny fingers extended from his hands like string beans. Still, he appeared healthy enough, if not downright cartoonish. He had on a fluffy scarf of made of cashmere and a silver suit cut to fit his slender frame. He held up one hand and put the other on his hips, as if he were posing for a magazine spread.

"And who the hell are you supposed to be?" I asked.

"My name is Einar Kjølaas," he replied in a thick Norwegian accent. "I am the architect who designed this place; Motherlove Headquarters, and The Impossible Room."

"Where the fuck did you come from?" I said.

He raised an eyebrow and said:

"Where the fuck did I come from, indeed!"

46

But back to the story of James Watson, and his newly formed clone.

Back to the basement of my father's house on Sycamore Lane.

The concoction before him bubbled up, like soda fizz. My father gasped and he leaned in closer. He could barely see me—hardly bigger than a pinhole—kicking around in the petri dish like a protozoa, like a single-celled thing.

But still, he had done it!

He had created life!

He had beaten the odds, defied logic, conquered his own biology, and parented a child!

It was me! I was that child! Hi!

He thought that perhaps he should celebrate. He thought he should call up ex-wife Petra so he could shout into the phone: "I did this! I did this all myself and I didn't need you at all, YOU WHORE!"

Of course, if he did call her, the words he would've actually shouted would've been something more along the lines of: "I'M SO ALONE AND NOBODY IN THIS UGLY WORLD CARES WHETHER I LIVE OR DIE AND I AM DR. FRANKENSTIEN I WILL BUILD YOU AN UNHOLY ABOMINATION IN A TEST TUBE IN MY BASEMENT TO PROVE TO YOU THAT I AM WORTHY OF YOUR LOVE."

He decided that maybe it'd be best not to call her at all.

47

Who he called, instead, was Dr. Anne.

"h—hello?" she answered the phone, her voice as raspy as the nighttime breeze.

"Dr. Anne?"

"Yes?"

"It's me, James. James Watson."

There was a pause.

"Who?"

"James Watson. From Motherlove Incorporated. Well, *formerly*, from Motherlove Incorporated. You handed me your card two weeks ago after our session. And you said '*call me if you need me.*' You said those exact words to me."

Another pause, and so he added: "I was the guy in the bathrobe covered in trash who you threatened to stab in the neck with a knife…"

"James, do you have any idea what time it is?"

She sounded angry. And tired. James thought, I bet she smells like warm bread when she sleeps.

"Is it late?" James asked. "My clock stopped working when it caught on fire in my front yard."

"Yes, it's late," Dr. Anne replied.

"I haven't left the basement in a while. I've been so busy, working, working, working. It's felt like one long day."

"What?"

She was on the verge of shouting. And so he said: "Dr.

Anne, I need your help…"

To which she dramatically rolled her eyes, a gesture that was lost in translation over the phone.

"Look, James, I really don't know what to tell you. It's the middle of the night and you're obviously in the middle of a manic episode or something. I have no idea what your deal is right now. And frankly, I don't care. I'd say contact me in the morning and we can discuss this in a more professional setting, but as you no longer work for Motherlove Incorporated and I'm under contract that my practice be limited to their offices and employees, legally-speaking, I can't even suggest that. My advice, then, would be to swallow whatever pills you have in your medicine cabinet and get some goddamn sleep."

"But Dr. Anne," my father said. "This is a matter of *life* and *death*!"

"Oh jeezus, James, what *isn't* a matter of life and death?" she replied. "Every minute of every day—it all seems so dire, so important, so finite—and yet, there's only two possible outcomes to every situation: Life or death. You live, or you die. How is a phrase like that supposed to contain any power when we're all in the process of either living or dying?"

James Watson didn't reply. He didn't have a snappy comeback or a clever rejoinder. He had nothing to offer, so he just breathed, heavily, into the receiver as the tears sloshed around in his eyes.

"I—I don't know who else to turn to," he eventually eked out just a decibel below a whisper. "I'm desperate. Please. I need you to come here…"

And Dr. Anne sighed the loudest and most audibly-exasperated sigh in the history of mankind, and said, "Okay, fine, I'll be over in a half hour then. Happy now, you big baby?"

48

Dr. Anne's silver hatchback pulled up to the curb in front of the house at the end of the cul-de-sac on Sycamore Lane. Above, the sun had dragged its purple tongue against the bottom of the horizon, preparing to chew its way out of the night. The sky glowed and a few early birds chirped. It was almost dawn when she arrived.

She surveyed the house. It looked like every other house on the block, completely innocuous, utterly unremarkable except for the black patch of charred grass in the front yard where my father had burned all of his possessions. She looked over her shoulder and could've sworn she saw two sets of glassy eyes watching her from the bedroom window in the Flatly's residence.

She hurried across the lawn and rang the doorbell.

James Watson answered, his eyes wild and wide and his face covered with sweat.

"Dr. Anne, thank you for coming."

"Holy shit, is that a screwdriver sticking out of your forehead?!?"

She reached out to touch it and my father grabbed her by the wrist and pulled his head away.

"Yes, it's in there, quite precariously I should add, and there's no telling what is going to happen if you start jiggling it around."

"Does it hurt?"

"Of course it hurts. It's a goddamn screwdriver in my goddamn head! But that's not why I called you here."

"It's not?"

"There are bigger things afoot, Dr. Anne. Please come in, come in..."

The doctor slowly stepped into James Watson's house.

She looked around at the empty walls, down empty halls; every room quiet, sterile, and bare, like an art museum in between exhibits.

"Where's all your stuff?" she asked.

"I burned it. I burned everything I owned."

Her shoes creaked against the floorboards. Every time she blinked, it sounded like a camera shutter. Even her breath had a reverb to it, echoing throughout the barren house.

They stopped in front of the basement door.

"Down here," he said, pulling it open on squeaky hinges.

"You want me to go down into your creepy basement?"

"It's not creepy," he said. "I swear."

He walked down the dusty stairs, Dr. Anne apprehensively following.

It was mostly dark. A dim 40-watt bulb hung from a string overhead, but the pallid light it gave was swallowed up by the edges of the room. Shadows encroached, thick like flannel sheets. In the dark corners, she pictured webs full of deadly spiders. It smelled of the earth, moss and mushrooms. There was a dampness down here too, and her skin was immediately coated with a clammy sheen.

The focus of the basement was an old wooden worktable, which was covered with an assortment of lights and laboratory equipment. A beaker of blue liquid fizzled under the flame of a Bunsen burner. Another tube of yellow fluid simmered nearby. There were microscopes and centrifuges and scraps of litmus paper. It all seemed to be in orbit around one particular petri dish.

She walked closer, looking down, seeing me for the first time, a bloody little half-formed zygote writhing in the sticky agony of my nascent existence. I don't know if I made a sound, but if I did I would imagine it would've been something close to a scream.

The good doctor gasped, brought a hand to her mouth, and looked at my father with terrified eyes.

"Alright fine, I'll admit it," said James, "The basement is a little creepy."

49

Years ago, long before my father's pregnancy, long before Dr. Caterwaul and his diagnoses tore his life asunder, there was James and ex-wife, Petra, who wasn't his ex-wife yet, and who wasn't even his wife yet, but rather she was just the girl he was dating.

They were young and they were still in love.

"Will you stay with me forever?" James asked her. They had just finished having sex, and the summertime breeze coming in through the window caressed their bare skin.

"Of course, my darling," Petra replied. "Why would you ask me such a silly thing?"

In that moment, anything seemed possible.

50

But back in the basement:

Dr. Anne shrieked and grabbed a nearby can of Raid, smashing the button down and spraying it on my twitching, unformed body. The amniotic goo around me fizzled up like a bloody wound that had just been doused by peroxide.

"What are you doing?!" my father shouted, knocking the can out of Dr. Anne's hand.

"What the hell is that thing?" she said. "What are you doing down here? What is this nightmare?"

She was backing away from him, slowly, eyes darting from the stairs to his face, and back to the stairs. Could she escape? Could she hit him and make a run for it, screaming, out into the night?

She pressed up against the wall. Cold, unmovable concrete behind her.

"Look, please, I need help…" he said.

"I'll say."

"No, I—I need a doctor. You're a doctor, right? Dr. Anne, that's your name. That makes you a doctor. I need someone to help us."

"What are you talking about, James? What do you mean *us*?"

He inhaled sharply and held his breath, then let the air pass audibly out through his nose. The tension deflated from his body as he exhaled, and he shrank a bit, seemed to collapse into himself, became less of a wolf and more of a puppy. He held out a hand for the terrified Dr. Anne.

She looked at it as one might look at an old rope bridge,

wondering if it's safe to cross. With little recourse, she eventually reached out and took it, letting him lead her over to the worktable.

"It's okay," he said. "I'm not crazy. I want to introduce you to someone…"

He pointed to the embryo, to me, trying to survive in my test tube womb.

"This is my son," he said. "This is Jimmy Watson Jr."

51

"James, I'm a psychologist, not a pediatrician. What do I know about biology? About babies? About…whatever the fuck it is you're doing down here."

That's what Dr. Anne said to my father as she sat on the basement steps and tried to process what he just asked of her.

"I'm not qualified for this," she said. "Don't you have a primary care physician or something?"

"No!" my father said. "Not him. He's full of bad news. If I called him up and said 'Dr. Caterwaul, I have a screwdriver sticking out of my head and I've cloned myself' he would probably say something like 'you are suffering from internal bleeding, and that creature growing under those table lights should be fed to an incinerator.' I know that's what he'd say and the clock on the wall would go *tick tick tick* and then he'd take the next patient and then the next patient and then the next, and when he's all out of patients for the day he'd drive his Lexus to the country club and tee off on the back nine and drink a highball and eat mozzarella sticks, and then one day I will die and I will be dead forever and the world will keep spinning around without me, and I'm just supposed to sit there in the chair across from him knowing all of this, and nod along like an idiot as he's saying to me IT'S TERMINAL TERMINAL TERMINAL, as if the desk between us and his diploma and all his degrees have somehow allowed him to escape the prison of his own body, like we're all not on the brink of losing our minds at any given moment, and our inevitable demise looms closer still, larger than life could ever be, all of life collectively—all the people to ever come and go from this world—larger than the sun and the moon and stars: DEATH, ETERNAL. Dr. Anne, you *really* want me to confront all of that, right now, when I can see, glowing inside of you, compassion like a broomstick to shoo away all these rats hiding in my soul? When we are standing here, on the precipice of a new day, about to break on through to whatever is on the other side? This is a moment, perhaps the most important moment I've ever experienced, and here I am, asking for nothing more than your unbiased ear to hear me out, and perhaps your competent hand to function in the ways that mine cannot."

She sat silent and thought about everything he just said to her.

"But James, I wouldn't even know where to begin…"

"I do," my father said. "I need you to put that baby inside me."

52

The plan was to impregnate my father with his own clone. With me.

There were a lot of logistical concerns to be addressed, of course. In this case especially, where ideation and reality were a canyon apart, you couldn't just say "I'm gonna impregnate myself with my own clone" and then wave your hands around like *abracadabra* and expect the impossible to have just magically happened. The male body does not typically come equipped with the biological processes that allow a developing human life to flourish inside of it. The two of them had to get creative, and luckily enough, James had been impaled through the forehead with a screwdriver and his brain was still crackling with the static-electric buzz of "good" ideas.

And sure, some may look at his behavior in these early days of my conception and call it mania. James Watson was psychotic, some might say. At the very least, unstable. And perhaps they'd be right. I always pictured his brain like a circuit breaker overheating, white sparks flying out of his ears, contrails of smoke rising from his nose. But the power stayed on. So we all continued to live in the house.

Okay, so what I'm going to do is break pregnancy down, problem-by-problem. Tackle them one at a time. Show you how it's done.

53

Problem #1: How did they keep my fetus from dying while they solved all of the other problems?

The two of them looked down at proto-me. Dr. Anne crossed her arms and pouted her lips. My father scratched his head and exhaled sharply.

"How have you kept him alive so far?" she asked.

"Well you see that pink shit he's wiggling around in?" he said.

"Yeah?"

"I figured he needed blood, right? And babies drink milk too, don't they? So I mixed the two of them together and poured it in there."

Coiled heat lamps glowed orange a few inches above my petri dish, like I was a bunch of fast food French fries he was trying to keep warm. The entire basement was uncomfortably warm. The viscous soup I was in was curdling.

"This isn't going to last. He's already getting crusty round the edges. He looks like an old booger in a bloody tissue," she said.

"Yes, we need to somehow…store him away until we're ready to put him inside of me."

Arm crossed tighter and lips pouted further. This was the tableau my parents always took when then were thinking. Problem-solving. Geniuses-at-work. And then, Dr. Anne's eyebrows jumped.

"I got it," she said as she grabbed her keys and ran up the stairs.

"Where are you going?" he shouted after her.

But she was already out the door.

It was morning by then. On a Tuesday. The neighbors were standing at the bus stop, waiting for the bus to the Motherlove Incorporated Building downtown. They all saw Dr. Anne run out, wet circles around her armpits, hair matted against her head, mascara smeared. If anybody recognized her from the office, they certainly didn't show it. The crooked looks she was offered had nothing to do with her capacity as a doctor and everything to do with her association with James Watson, who's downward spiral was not only whispered, but on constant display. The Flatlys and Mosses figured her for a prostitute who had just narrowly escaped being shanked.

Anyway, she went to the nearby grocery store and picked up a few packs of watermelon Jell-O.

When she returned, she was no longer apprehensive as she trod across my father's soot-covered lawn. Her steps were confident, and direct. The horror inside that house didn't lurk in the shadows anymore. The horror was growing in plain view, under heat lamps, and betwixt the wrinkles of my father's sparkling brain. The horror was named Jimmy Watson Jr., and he had shared it with her because it was his only gift to give.

She went to his kitchen and boiled the Jell-O up and then poured it into a…

"Do you have any Tupperware? Bowls? Do you have any type of container in here at all?" she shouted out to my father.

"I think they all got burned up," he shouted back, from the basement.

And so she took off her shoe and poured the Jell-O into it and then her and my father dumped my zygote (amniotic syrup and all) into the quivering crimson mass. I floated in the center of it as it began to solidify, until I was completely held in stasis, like an insect in amber.

They slipped the shoe into the refrigerator, putting me in a makeshift cryogenic sleep until they could figure out what to do next.

54

Problem #2: Where was a fetus supposed to go, inside my father's body?

The male body wasn't biologically structured to carry a child inside of it.

But you knew that...right? I HOPE this isn't new information.

Point is, were they to stick my developing fetus inside my father without taking proper precautions, his white blood cells would've surely descended upon and dissolved me long before I had my first cognizant thought, and then this sad comedy would end on this very page. And that would be that. And I know that wouldn't be a particularly satisfying conclusion to this story, no, but sometimes neutrality is the best-case-scenario.

55

But Dr. Anne was clever, and she solved Problem #2, like the problem prior, with relatively little effort.

First, they had to encase my fetus in something to protect it from the harmful bacterium inside my father's body; an amniotic sac of sorts, in which I could safely develop. Once again, she relied on the nearby grocery store for inspiration, this time taking my father with her so that the two of them could peruse the shelves together like expectant parents wandering the aisles of Babies 'R Us. They eventually stopped in the meat department, picking up a fresh length of pork sausage.

Back at the house, Dr. Anne used her delicate hands to squeeze the meat out of the casing. *Plop,* the uncooked flesh landed in the sink in a fatty pile.

"Now get the shoe," Dr. Anne instructed my father.

He removed my makeshift womb from the refrigerator.

The transfer from shoe to sausage casing was inelegant at best, Dr. Anne holding the casing like a used condom, my father using a teaspoon to shovel me and the watermelon Jell-O around me into it. When he was done, he licked the spoon clean.

"Waste not, want not," he said with a wink.

"Okay, now lay down," she said.

"Lay down? Right here?" asked James, motioning to the kitchen counter.

"Do you have an operating suite set-up somewhere you haven't told me about yet?"

"No…"

"Then here is fine."

He climbed up on the counter and lay flat on his back. Dr. Anne lifted his shirt. His belly jiggled as the fabric rubbed against it and, instinctively, a bashful James Watson went to pull it back down. Dr. Anne slapped his hand.

"Ow!"

"You weren't shy a few weeks ago in my office when you were in just your underwear, covered in rotten food."

"I thought I was dying then," he said.

"And you're condition has somehow been miraculously cured?" she scoffed. "You're going to be the only human being in the history of mankind to live forever?"

He pointed at the screwdriver in his forehead. "Things are under control for the moment."

She lifted his shirt again and poured some liquid soap over his lower stomach, focusing on an area about and two inches to the left and one inch above his navel. He giggled.

"It tickles," he said.

"This is a medical procedure," she said, removing the large, sharp knife from their therapy session from her handbag. "Stop smiling."

"Do you know what you're doing?" he asked.

"No new parent ever does," she replied.

And she stabbed him in the stomach.

56

Ice-cream thick blood poured out of the puncture wound.

My father winced, sucked in air through his teeth. It puddled beneath him, pooling up and running over the edge of the counter in red streaks.

"Damn, that stings," he said. "There seems to be a lot of blood. Did you cut an artery? Should I be bleeding this much? What do you see in there?"

"Can you shut up? I'm trying to concentrate," she said.

"Sorry."

She placed the knife down and dug her fingers into the incision, prying the fissure open wider. Even more blood squirted out in crimson fountains, pink chunks of flesh and fat getting caught up in the current before being ejected against the kitchen wall.

James Watson's had gone pale. Tears streamed down his cheeks. Bile climbed up his throat and leaked out of his nose.

"Okay, this part might hurt a bit," Dr. Anne said as she grabbed up a handful of spaghetti-shaped guts and pulled it out of the hole in his body. Picking the knife up once again, she moved quickly, lopping off a piece of intestine about three inches long. It landed in the sink, next to the pork meat, almost indistinguishable from the rest of the slop.

She then took the baby-filled sausage casing and inserted it into the empty space in his intestine, replacing the section she just removed. A small, round piece of screen door was placed on either end as a catch, to keep my father's digestive system from flushing my fetus out with the rest of his waste. A dab of boat glue on either end was enough to hold the slippery Jell-O stuffed tube in place until it could heal over more permanently.

This was my new womb.

Dr. Anne was sweating profusely. Her nostrils flared and she had barely let out a breath during the entire procedure. Having no medical training whatsoever put her at a serious disadvantage when performing this surgery. But it appeared to have been successful.

She glued his stomach shut and raised her hands triumphantly, like she just scored a goal in a soccer match.

"Done!" she shouted, finally exhaling.

"Can I sit up?" asked James.

"Um…yeah, I guess? Just…be slow. It's healing."

James swung his feet around and sat upright. I sloshed around in his belly. I was jolted. I bounced against the sides of his intestines. It made my father ill. Morning sickness. Before he could get to his feet he puked up some brown gunk into the sink. Then he turned back to Dr. Anne. She could hear his heart quicken as a smile spread across his face, rusty vomit caked between his crooked teeth.

"I'm so fucking happy," he said.

57

I spent the first few months of my development surrounded completely by my father's waste.

I had no other choice. His intestinal tract was also my umbilicus.

The screen doors that Dr. Anne had inserted on either side of my womb kept my body from being swept away in the river of excreta, but it didn't stop the excreta from being swept past me.

Without those tiny screen doors, I would've surely been miscarried out of my father's anus. I would've been nothing but a bloody stool, never born, passed through this world as simply and as effortlessly as a fart. The ghosts of all the people who never came to be certainly outnumber the ghosts of those who have come and perished. And I could've been one of them. The universe has infinitely more *maybes* than *yeses* and *nos*.

The top screen kept out most of the solid matter, so as not to let it compact and crush my delicate, half-formed bones. Of course, this caused the feces to collect up in my father's large intestine. With no way to purge itself from his body, it ballooned up inside of him like a massive boil about to rupture.

This was *Problem #3: What to do with my father's shit, and the interruption and/or reconfiguration of any of his normal biological imperatives?*

58

Dr. Anne had stayed at my father's house ever since the morning of the operation.

She had been there about a week or so, spending the nights in a pile of rags on the empty floor of an empty room down an empty hallway on the second story.

"Are you sure you don't want a...ya know, bed or something?" my father said to her, the bubble on his stomach above me swollen up with rotten stool. "I burned up my old one, but we can order a new one. They sell beds on the internet, right? We'll have some guys deliver it."

"I'll be fine, James," she said. "It's YOU that I'm worried about. Someone needs to monitor your progress, and figure out how to keep both you, and your son, alive."

"I thought you weren't that kind of doctor."

"I'm not," she said.

And then, seven days after my conception, my father was experiencing a feverish illness. A week's worth of fecal matter had metastasized next to me, in his small intestine. His skin had jaundiced and his body temperature spiked. He slipped in and out of consciousness.

Dr. Anne dealt with this issue, and all issues, as they arrived. She pondered solutions and tested hypothesis. And she solved Problem #3 in the most practical way possible: by installing a relief valve directly into James Watson's guts.

It looked like one of those hose hookups you'd find on the

side of a house, a metal spigot with an octagonal handle which he could turn and drain every time the pressure built up or he got too full of solid matter. The spigot poked out of him about an inch, just above the hip, rusty and crooked. He wore a belly shirt, so he could easily access to it.

Liquid waste still passed through the screen and evacuated his body in the traditional way. Aqueous excreta would wash over me like muddy water in an overflowing storm drain. The Jell-O that had originally encased me dissolved quickly, and throughout the rest of my father's pregnancy, this sludge was the only thing I had to feed on. From one generation to the next, eating his shit.

59

Many years before this story began, Dr. Anne was once engaged to a man. His name didn't matter much now, it was just a regular name anyway, something normal, like Bill.

He was a charmer, though. He said all the right things at all the right times. He swept her off her feet, and her heart became unbound. She got lost in him. She fell in love.

One day, he fucked a knobby-kneed intern from his office cluster, hip deep in her young body, Dr. Anne scarcely a thought in his head. It was just the kind of guy he was. And so that was the end of that.

These days Dr. Anne abhorred such a naïve and hyperbolic phrase: *He swept her off her feet*. Like love was this unstoppable wave, crashing violently upon her shores. Love filling her lungs with sea water. Love irrepressible, like The Gray Tide itself. The words were poetic, yes, they conjured images of beauty, but they were also banal and deceptive and hollow. Poetry alone won't save anyone.

Point is, if you called her a hopeless romantic, she'd probably scoff at you, roll her eyes, throw up a delicate hand and stop you midsentence: "I'm a pragmatist," she'd say. "And my position as Motherlove's resident psychologist demands that I approach all things in a measured and rational way."

She'd say to you: "Love is just a mammalian drive—as innate and cruel as hunger—obligatory for the survival and propagation of the species."

She'd say: "Love is clinical, diagnosable, the same as any other disease."

But:

When she was a little girl, her mother read her fairy tales. As a teenager, she watched meet-cute comedies like *The Wedding Singer* and *Never Been Kissed*. As a young woman, she slept with many people, searching through them for something indefinable. And now, as a lonely adult, her bookshelves full of harlequin romance novels, pages dog-eared, spines bent and cracked. As pragmatic as she fancied herself to be, when her fiancée absconded away with his intern, he took a piece of Dr. Anne's heart with him. She was left with a void within herself she neither asked for, nor understood.

"I deserve good things, don't I?" she would wonder, in her most private moments. In the shower or in bed at night, in those quiet places where skepticism was stretched its thinnest.

She didn't know it then, on that first night there, as she made a bed of rags on the floor in the guest room of my father's house, but the two of them were already in the process of falling deeply, chaotically, apocalyptically in love.

And it would eventually destroy her.

Because that's what love does.

60

And at Motherlove, at present:

"Before we continue on," I said, "I need you to acknowledge that I am your king."

"You are my king," the flamboyantly dressed architect Einar Kjølaas conceded with an exaggerated bow.

"Say out loud that I am in charge of everything that you see..."

"You, sir, are in charge of the sun and the moon and the comets and the Earth."

It was a little over-the-top. Perhaps he was even mocking me, considering the Earth was literally crumbling apart beneath our feet. But I let it go. I am a benevolent ruler.

The garish man didn't appear anxious or fearful, which is strange considering the dire circumstances we've found ourselves in. Instead, he radiated confidence the way a car engine radiates heat. I couldn't make sense of it. Does he not fear The Tide? Even under my mantle of authority, I could feel the cracks covering my veneer, matching the cracks that crept up the foundation of the Motherlove Incorporated Building.

But Einar Kjølaas seemed almost bored as he plopped down in a chair and crossed his legs, lighting up a long, skinny cigarette. He looked like an anemic Andy Warhol, a sickly stick figure with wild hair and wilder eyes. Two wispy plumes of smoke coiled out of his nose. He smiled wide. His teeth were large and yellow.

"How did you get in here?" I asked. "Why aren't you dead,

like everyone else? Why hasn't your body been consumed by The Tide?"

"Fairest King of Motherlove, I am the one who designed this entire building. I am the one who designed The Impossible Room around us. I know all the ways in and out."

61

If textbooks were still being printed, if schools were still in session, if you could still open up Wikipedia and click on the article attached to my name, you would find me credited as the creator of The Gray Tide. It would read something along the lines of:

"*Jimmy Watson Jr. was an American inventor, chemist, and former head of research and development for Motherlove Incorporated, often cited with the discovering the mathematical formula from which both the anti-entropic drug Infinitassium, and the transglobal biological disaster The Gray Tide, were both synthesized. He is widely considered responsible for the end of the world* [citation needed]. "

Then there'd be my stupid little photo next to a picture of the half-eaten Earth.

62

There's a black spot on my brain, too, in case you were wondering.

It's my inheritance. My birth rite. My genetic cross to bear.

I can feel it inside my head, like James Watson must have felt it inside his, digging its claws into my cerebellum, rooting itself into my thoughts like weeds.

The same black spot cuts though the collective mind of The Gray Tide. I have more in common with the apocalypse than I wish to acknowledge.

63

So Einar Kjølaas raised an eyebrow and fluttered his lashes.

I cleared my throat.

"You, um, you said...you know of all the ways in and out of this place?"

He snuffed out his cigarette on the desk next to him and sprung up to his feet.

"Indeed I do, Your Majesty. And I might have a solution that could save us all, if you're open to hearing it."

I looked to my three (and only) other subjects: my wife, my assistant, and my accountant. Helen shrugged, as if to say, might as well hear him out. When Einar Kjølaas smiled at her, his torpedo-shaped jaw appeared even pointer. Maybe I'm just being paranoid. Armageddon will do that to a man. If he didn't want to help us, then why would he make himself known? What ulterior motives could he possibly have?

And so I said: "Go on..."

"This room," the architect said. "This impossible and infinite room, in which we currently hide. You look around it, and what do you see?"

"Some chairs?" offered Carol.

"Yes, what else?"

"A coffeemaker?" said Kelsey.

"A coffeemaker, sure, what else?"

"Cubicles," said Helen, the queen, my wife.

"Yes!" Einar Kjølaas danced as he talked, wiggling his hips

and tossing around his head. "Cubicles, twisting and winding chaotically about. They weave around each other. Crissing and crossing and crissing again..."

"Excuse me, but what is the point of all this, Mr. Kjølaas," I interrupted him.

"Are you familiar with matryoshka dolls, Mr. Watson?" he said.

"Of course I am!" I said, although I had no idea what he was talking about.

"Russian nesting dolls," he clarified, as if he could read my mind. "You have a wooden doll, hollow in its interior, and inside of it, you stick a second, smaller doll. And then, inside that doll, you place a third. And inside the third, there sits a fourth. In the fourth, a fifth. In the fifth, a sixth. And so on and so on and so on, until you can't make your dolls any smaller."

"I told you I already know what a...*marshabrady* doll is," I said. "But I don't see what you're getting at..."

"Well, what is this room –this office without borders– but a massive matryoshka doll?" he said.

He pulled another cigarette out of the breast pocket of his blazer and put it in the holder. He lit it up and inhaled deeply.

"And what do you posit would happen," he continued, "if I were to take my blueprints for The Impossible Room and scale them down, modify them, ever so slightly, and build a second, smaller Impossible Room, inside of this one? Another infinite office, inside the infinite office we're in right now. Surely it would take The Gray Tide some time to cross such an unfathomable expanse. And we would double it, just like that. And then, Mr. Watson..."

"King Jimmy," I corrected him.

"My apologies. So then, *King Jimmy*, what do you think would happen if, inside that newer, second office, I were to build another one? A third impossible room. And then another one after that? Smaller and smaller we'd go, wouldn't we? Nesting rooms within rooms, universes upon universes, infinities inside infinities. And if we go deep enough, if we travel down, down, down, and further down still, we *might* just be able to get away from this condemned place, forever."

He finished with his hands in the air, like a revival tent preacher right after the hymnal had its crescendo. The rest of us exchanged incredulous glances. And so I said:

"Well this is all good in theory, Mr. Kjølaas, but how would any of that protect us from The Gray Tide? When the ground gives out beneath the building, and The Tide besieges the walls, and the weight of all of those wretched creatures gets too great and whole thing implodes in on itself like a collapsing star, all these rooms will collapse inward, with it with us inside. Even infinity would be able to stop it."

"Stop it?" chuckled Einar Kjølaas. "No, no, no, Mr. Watson, I'm not trying to *stop* it. I can no more stop The Tide than YOU can, and we both know any attempt to do so would be a futile as it would be lofty. If even kings can't avoid death, then little men like me surely stand no chance. So no, I can't stop it. But what we can do is buy ourselves time. Push The Tide to the other side of the room. We can take whatever moments we have left –be they minutes or days or decades or whatever– and we can stretch them out, long like taffy, and rest them on the horizon of the next dawning day. We can run."

"And then what?"

"And then what *what*?" he said. "There is no then what. That's it, Mr. Watson. That's the end of the line."

My brow was furrowed.

"So you're saying, we go inward?" I asked.

"We get smaller," he answered.

"And it's not a permanent solution."

"Nothing is."

"But we might live to see tomorrow?" I said.

"And perhaps, if we're lucky, the day after that!" he said back.

64

Carol in accounting crunched the numbers.

Her fingers worked the calculator like she was a concert pianist, lithe and precise. She hit the 'equals' button, turned, and gave me a little nod. We could afford him. Because Einar Kjølaas services did not come cheap, and he refused to waive or amend his fees. Even under the circumstances we were currently facing, he expected to get paid.

Who could blame him?

When I was 18, I sold the first of James Watson's formulas to Motherlove Incorporated.

Who could blame me?

Back then:

The eggheads in Pharmaceuticals seemed to think there was quite a bit of potential in my father's scribblings. I mean *ahem* MY scribblings. They wanted to see more.

I said: "Sure, lemme see what I can do!"

I'd take a few weeks before I gave them another page. I had to pretend like I was hard at work.

"How's it coming Jimmy?" they'd ask.

"It'sa comin'," I'd cheekily reply. "You can't rush inspiration."

And after what felt like an appropriate amount of waiting time, I would emerge from my cubicle with a "new" equation, or some crude geometry, or an anatomically troubling drawing, or just a bunch of random numbers tied together by whatever the fuck these $\{\aleph \; \emptyset \; \propto \; \partial\}$ symbols meant. I couldn't make heads or tails of this stuff. But these nerds could.

"It's rough," the lead scientist told me, perusing the papers I had just handed the team. "Sloppy work. Some may even call it manic. You are not a man who understands biology, or physiology, or…anything really. Not in the traditional sense, at least. Still, the basic ideas you present are sound, if not over-the-top. We might be able to squeeze this lemon a bit, see if we can't make ourselves a little lemonade."

And sure enough, lemonade was made.

When the notes proved to be surprisingly fruitful, Motherlove quickly promoted me to the department head. I was in charge of the entire Research and Development Division, even though I had little to show myself in terms of research and/or development. But it was the end result that mattered most, so no one cared that I merely showed up one day with my father's formulas stuffed in my pocket like a first-class ticket, an ace-in-the-hole, a fastpass to the front of the line. One of the cigar-chopping CEO once laid it out in plain English:

"You just keep providing us with these fresh ideas, Jimmy, and we'll make sure you never have to worry about anything ever again."

And so I did just that. I brought James Watson's notebook to Motherlove Incorporated, passing it off as my own, and I let the fine folks in the white lab coats do whatever it is they did with it:

Create Infinitassium. Cure death. Engineer the end of the world.

And I got paid. You better believe I got paid.

I bought myself a car. No more bus rides for this breadwinner. My suits were sewn from Swiss Voile cotton. My shoes were handmade in Italy. My haircut cost $42. Eventually, I bought a decently-sized house in a suburb far away from Sycamore Lane. I took nice vacations to the kinds of places they would advertise for on billboards. I drank expensive scotch in the evenings when I was in a scotch-drinking mood.

65

If I were dictating this book to a ghostwriter, if this were a memoir of sorts, here is where I would have taken a lengthy pause and exhaled slowly before leaning in and saying something along the lines of, "I just want to state, for the record, that I didn't do it all for the money. The money certainly didn't hurt, of course, but that wasn't my only motivation."

And the ghostwriter, ready to plod into the darkest depths of the human psyche, would be compelled to ask me something like, "Well what else is there, King Jimmy?"

And I'd say, "There is another factor which often weighs heavy in the hearts of men, and it drove my father and Dr. Anne forward, as surely and steadily as it has driven me…"

And the ghostwriter would say, "And what is that?"

And I would say, "I'm talking about LOVE!

66

Now if it were Dr. Anne who was dictating her life story to a ghostwriter, and they were to ask her "When did you realize that you were in love with James Watson?" she'd probably laugh in a good-natured way before saying something along the lines of: "Well it certainly wasn't the first time I had to drain a bucket of shit out of his abdominal spigot!"

67

In order to fall in love with a man like my father, you must think a woman like Dr. Anne had been damaged in the past, broken in some convoluted way. As if our personalities were just jagged puzzle pieces that providence had cut out for only one another. But it's not as simple as all that. Proclamations don't always come at you bold-faced and underlined. Trauma isn't exclusive to the least fortunate among us, and sadness isn't the purview of a disenfranchised few.

We're all going to die. It's big and black and it's right there in front of us, its bony finger beckoning us forward whether we choose to acknowledge it or not.

It's enough to drive the sanest person mad.

And yet, we all face it.

And somehow carry on.

68

Now, at this junction, our hypothetical ghostwriter might think it was prudent to relay a quick anecdote about Dr. Anne's childhood to you.

"This will help further elucidate and illustrate her character arc and reinforce the statements that were just made about her," he might say.

How very academic of him!

And even though the language and scenery he uses are abstract, even though he may employ some 'poetic licensing' to fill in all the gaps and smooth out the rough edges, even though this short diversion doesn't necessarily drive the narrative forward in any significant way, it doesn't matter. He is the one writing the book right now. If you're looking symbolism here, you're free to ascribe meaning at will. There's plenty to latch on to. For the rest of you who only enjoy things at face-value (and there's nothing wrong with that!) at least, entertainment-wise, this parable should suffice:

Dr. Anne wasn't always a doctor. At one point, she was just Annie, a 9-year-old girl who loved animals more than anything else. Before she grew up and decided to devote her professional life to psychology, she wanted to be a veterinarian.

She would spend her days reading books on taxonomy she borrowed from the library, and she'd peruse articles about biology in the encyclopedia. She was an obsessive child, with a singular purpose. Surely, she had always been this way. To this day both curiosity and infatuation pilot her decision-making almost as much as reason does.

Her favorite animal was the giraffe. She had seen one in the zoo, on a school field trip, and had become totally enamored with it. She learned everything she could about the animal; its diet, habitat, mating habits, its psychical and mental characteristics.

"Can we get a giraffe?" not-yet-doctor Annie asked her mother one night at the dinner table.

"I don't think you're allowed to keep giraffes as pets," her mother replied.

"Well, we just won't tell anyone. We'll hide it. No one will know."

"We'll hide a giraffe?"

"Yes."

"What about your cat?"

"What about him?"

"Don't you like your cat anymore?"

"He scratched me!"

"He's a cat, honey, that's what he does."

Young Annie didn't like that answer, of course. She stormed out of the kitchen and went to her room, stomping her feet like they were little anvils. She slammed the door behind her in a huff.

"Stupid mom…" she muttered to herself.

"Meow?" said the cat, slowly climbing out from underneath her bed.

Annie went to pet it and it scratched her. She frowned.

Downstairs, her mother cleared the kitchen table, did the dishes, wiped the counter, swept the floor. She looked around the now-clean kitchen and, making sure her child was not in the room, pulled a Marlboro Light out of a crumpled box in the junk drawer. She lit a match, but right before she touched the flame to the end, there was an awful wail that emanated from the other side of the house. It was loud, ululating, terrified, tortured, wrung from the lungs of something in excruciating pain.

"Annie!" her mother yelled, the unlit cigarette falling from her lips to the spotless linoleum floor.

More screaming, then the cat yowling, enough to shake the windows and vibrate the walls.

Her mother ran down the hallway and threw open her daughter's bedroom door. She gasped. Little Annie had cut off the cat's head.

The young girl stood there, still holding the knife, blood sprayed across the walls, pooled up beneath them in syrupy puddles.

But not just that:

Annie had also cut off her own left arm, somehow severing the limb at the shoulder joint. Crimson slime leaked down the side of her tiny body, staining the pastel blue sundress she wore. Her mother stifled the urge to vomit.

Annie had then taken her arm and somehow "attached" it to the stump where the cat's neck had been cleaved. Crude stitches held the arm in place, dripping white globules from the fissure where the two bodies met, like she had squirted some Elmer's glue in there to reinforce the surgery.

The human limb on the cat body bobbed at the elbow, reached down and scooped the detached kitten head from the floor. Holding it tight, like a pitcher holding a baseball, the tips of her fingers digging under the skin, behind its ears and up the side of its face.

This monstrosity hobbled drunkenly over to her mother, its paws lightly treading through the splattered gore. Annie's mother's heart raced, her breath was arrested. She could only look on in sheer horror as the cat slowly opened its eyes and looked around, before fixing its gaze on the woman's terrified face, opening its mouth, and going: "Meow."

"I did it," said Annie, a big smile on her rosy cheeks. "I built myself a giraffe."

69

They reattached Dr. Anne's arm, in case you were wondering. You couldn't even tell it had been removed in the first place.

And what happened to the cat, you ask?

Well, what do you think?

70

So Dr. Anne cautiously, but steadily, moved into the Watson house: one outfit, one sundry, one small piece of herself at a time. Before she even realized what was happening, the lease on her old apartment had lapsed and now she resided completely with my father at the end of the cul-de-sac on Sycamore Lane.

She still worked at Motherlove Incorporated, as their in-house psychologist. For the time being, at least. One day, she would just stop going into there, too, as her responsibilities at home took up more and more of her time.

On the days she went into the office, an increasingly pregnant-with-me James Watson fixed up the house he once destroyed. He refurbished the table and reupholstered a couch. He mowed the lawn and mopped the floor. He dusted and swept and polished and washed.

His waistline expanded. I swelled up in him like a plum. Then from a plum, I grew into a cantaloupe, and from a cantaloupe, a watermelon I became. Dangling, the flesh stretched and thin, almost translucent. A backlight would've surely exposed my developing skeleton latched to his intestine, sucking whatever nutrients I could acquire from the liquid shit washing over me.

The pregnancy had an ameliorative effect on my father. In those moments, he found a mental peace he had previously never considered possible. Was it simply a case of this slew of new hormones flowing through him, latent chemicals coming unglued from sticky synapses, changing his perspective in such a subtle yet profound way? Probably. But that doesn't make it pretend. Even if it was only temporary. And although the black spot in his brain still quivered, still spread, still pulsated and squeezed around the screwdriver's stem, the period of my gestation would be, as my father later told me, one of the happiest times of his life, an experience never replicable with the pregnancies of any of my brothers.

On the back porch one evening, as the daylight turned to night, James Watson stood, content with the sound of the wind tussling the tops of the trees. Dr. Anne passed through the slider door and stood next to him, laying her hands on his malformed baby bump.

"It would seem impossible," she said. "All of this is impossible, and yet, here we are, together. It's almost…a miracle."

And that was when they shared their first kiss.

To that ghostwriter, James Watson might say:

"Perhaps, in that moment, I was naïve. But it felt good, and goodness was a feeling I was unfamiliar with. So I let it run away with me. I surrendered myself to it. Somewhere, deep down inside, I knew that the birth of Jimmy wasn't going to 'fix' me. And I knew that a woman like Dr. Anne wasn't put on this Earth to act as a bandage for my endlessly bleeding sores. Whatever incurable and rotten hold the black spot had on me was a burden from which there would never truly be an escape. Still, in that ephemeral moment at least, life was overflowing from me, both literally and symbolically. Do you understand what it's like? I had so much love inside me that I didn't know what to do with it all. How could I have known that something as pure as love could turn you into toxic waste if you imbibe too much of it? I didn't know it even could, let alone *would* destroy me. In the end, love is an affliction. A curse. Love killed me."

71

One day soon after:

Dr. Anne came home with a print of a framed painting that she bought from an art store in the mall. A gift for my father. A surprise.

She hung it on the wall above his workbench in the basement.

James walked down the stairs, saw it, and stopped.

"What is this?" he said as he stared at the image.

In the painting: there was a bunch of clocks, melting, on the barren shores of some muddy costal beach. One clock was loosely draped over the branch of a tree. Another was sliding down the side of a table. Still another was limply lain on top of some kind of white fleshy mass, perhaps part of a face?

It was aesthetically repulsive. Jarring. Visceral. Unnerving. It was not the calming abstract art you'd find in corporate offices buildings and hotel room halls. This was surreal. This thing demanded that you look at it, whether you wanted to or not.

"It's called *The Persistence of Memory*," she said. "By Salvador Dali. I thought you might like to, I dunno, spruce up this dank room a little bit."

"I don't get it," he said.

"Don't get what?"

"Why are those clocks melting?"

"Um…well…." she said, sidling up next to him and taking his hand into hers, "some people seem to think they represent entropy, the inevitable decline of all things, from order to disorder. As the clocks lose their rigidity, so does our concept of the rigidity of time. And without time, there's no order. We are drawn into the mud, into the landscape itself, as are all things."

"Odd that an artist would try to represent decay with a fixed image, such as a painting. Here, disorder is frozen, solidified in bold colors upon a cotton canvas. I could blink a thousand times, and this picture would be the same every time I reopened my eyes."

"Well we use the tools we can find and work in whatever medium we can," she said.

"Are you afraid of the future, Dr. Anne?" he asked her after a moment's pause.

"Of course," she said. "But I think that's kind of the point. That we stand here and look at this ugly thing and ask ourselves what it all means. It's up to us to ultimately decide."

"So what are you saying? That there's no delineation between questions and answers? That all we have are pictures in between? And that things are already falling apart, even as we try to build them?"

"Yeah, something like that."

PART THREE:

BIRTH, AND ALL THE THINGS THAT HAPPENED AFTER THAT

72

I was born on a Saturday.

It was a day like any other. Except that this time, it wasn't.

My father had gone into labor in the middle of Brad and Jennifer Flatly's weekly backyard barbeque.

This had been the first barbeque my father attended in almost a year. The first one since he had his...*ahem*...little breakdown, however many chapters ago that was. Somewhere near the beginning of the book. You remember that scene, right? Where he screamed and cried and tore up grass as he pathetically crowed out again and again 'woe is me, woe is me, woe woe woe?'

He had come a long way since then.

73

Brad and Jennifer Flatly, upon seeing him now, could barely recognize the troubled neighbor they once thought they knew. And this was not just because James Watson was 9-months pregnant. There are plenty of pregnant people out there who look the same as they always did.

No, it was because on that particular Saturday, James Watson was all-smiles, the rarest configuration for his often-dour face.

On that Saturday my father smiled as he listened to Brad talk about some article he read in the local newspaper, as he talked about sports, about politics, about the boring-ass weather; as Brad talked about normal people stuff.

74

James Watson had a mouthful of potato salad when, all of a sudden, the contractions began.

Perhaps under ordinary circumstances, this would've meant a somewhat frantic car ride to the local maternity ward. But birth for a man was not a natural process by any means, and delivering this child was a procedure that no hospital was prepared to do.

The thing was: James Watson's tubes and veins and vessels were all tangled up, rerouted and detoured, jumbled beyond medical recognition. Inserting my fetus into his body had caused a traffic jam in his arteries and forced his insides to restructure themselves. And so, as labor suddenly began, blood leaked out through all of his pores at once. In a matter of minutes, he was soaked in red. It spilled out of his nose and ears, hemorrhaged out of the bottom of his eyelids. Poured from his mouth. Sweat out of his pits. He screamed as the fetal sac protruding from the side of his stomach started to split open and my pointy head came poking out.

75

Earlier though:

There was hamburgers and hot dogs and citronella candles and a horseshoe pit. There was music on the stereo, not a specific album, but the local classic rock radio station, playing all of the hits. The whole cul-de-sac was there. Brad and his wife Jennifer hosting. Harrison and Tabitha Moss, from across the way, bringing refreshments.

James and Dr. Anne arrived at the time Brad had told them to. Dr. Anne even brought a bowl of watermelon Jell-O.

They all sat around a patio table, underneath a large brown umbrella, even though it was already after dark. Moths fluttered around the porchlight. Crickets chirped in the bushes.

"Beer?" Brad offered James a drink, holding out a cold can of domestic pilsner.

"Oh no," said my father, resting his hand on his stomach. "I shouldn't."

"Oh right," Brad elbowed Harrison and chuckled. "Jamesy here is watching his figure."

"No, Brad, I told you before, I haven't gotten fat. I'm pregnant."

"Ah, that's right, I keep forgetting."

76

And even earlier than that:

James and Dr. Anne had considered not going to the barbeque at all. They had debated it, as couples do. They said: let's stay in, let's fall asleep on the couch, let's not be social, let's let it slip our minds. What would it've really mattered anyway? James Watson's neighbors served no noble function in his story. When The Gray Tide came they remained side characters, truly, until the bitter end.

Because the truth was, James Watson didn't have the TIME for side characters. He already felt the pull, back down to his basement, to the place where he momentarily found power and solace in my creation. To him, *that's* what made sense. *That's* where he belonged. *That* was the point. The rest of this was... just a distraction.

His obsession could be blamed on the black spot, of course, a symptom of the death sentence he carried inside his head. Dr. Caterwaul would've surely said so, with all the bedside manner of a porcupine:

"Man, you are totally fuuuuuuuuuuuuuuuucked," the mustached doctor would've said.

And Dr. Anne might've agreed:

"Maybe our relationship should remain professional only," she would've said, "I can't get romantically involved with someone who is so totally fuuuuuuuuuuuuuuuucked."

It's crazy to think how easy it is for epic love stories to

slip right by us, to never get told, all because the two main characters decided their first chance encounter didn't warrant a second one.

Or maybe the problem wasn't the black spot at all. Maybe we can pin this on the screwdriver that was still sticking out of the center of his forehead, like a radio tower, picking up signals from space. Yes, maybe there was something cosmic going on here. Something revelatory and divine. Something shamanic. Maybe everything that was about to transpire was inescapable. Maybe my father was just one finger on the hand of God, ready to smite and smash this wicked world to pieces.

Hmmm, I suppose that would make me a finger too, wouldn't it?

Maybe we're all the fingers of God. Maybe life is nothing more than His mighty fist.

77

So pregnant James Watson was distracted by these thoughts, both practical and abstract, while his haplessly smiling mouth was full of potato salad at the backyard barbeque at the house next door. And there was Brad Flatly, prattling on and on about his new something-or-other in the garage. A leaf blower, perhaps? Really, Brad? Who could possibly care about a fucking leaf blower at a time like this? Don't you know there are questions about the universe that are still unanswered?

And as Brad was saying something along the lines of "blah blah blah blah blah blah blah" all of James Watson's muscles went weak. He slid out of his seat and onto the patio. The contractions came on suddenly, as if he were cast by a spell. One minute he was sitting there, and the next he was on the floor, blood and pink pus pouring out of all of his orifices.

Jennifer Flatly and Tabitha Moss let out a synchronized gasp. If they had pearls around their necks, they would've surely been clutched. Brad and Harrison leapt up from their seats, throwing their hands up in shock like their bleeding neighbor just performed some kind of morbid magic trick.

Dr. Anne stopped midsentence. One moment she was saying something mundane like "Yes we were thinking of planting arugula in the garden, as it's supposed to be high in antioxidants and vitamin C." And the next she's screaming "HOLY FUCK MY BOYFRIEND IS SQUIRTING FOUNTAINS OF BLOOD FROM HIS EYEHOLES AND

GIVING BIRTH TO HIS CLONE RIGHT NOW!"

She dropped to her knees and cradled my father.

"He's going into labor," she shouted at the befuddled neighbors.

"We shouldn't be looking at this!" Harrison Moss cried out. "Everyone, avert your eyes! This is unnatural It's not possible! It's...un-Christian!"

Dr. Anne ignored the raving man as she grabbed James Watson by his feet and dragged him across the patio, leaving a snail trail of pink, gooey slime behind him. Ejecta squirted from every opening in his body, gory refuse dribbled from every pore. He screamed in agony. She screamed in fear.

She made it halfway across the street before he dug his heels into the pavement, halting her. She slipped and fell down in front of him, covered in sweat and blood, looking like she just climbed out of a red swimming pool. It was there, in the center of the cul-de-sac at the end of Sycamore Lane, that the embryonic sac attached to the side of my father's hip, like a canteen full of fetal scraps, split open and out I fell.

The sun shone down that day.

The moon could also be seen, faintly.

I screamed my way into the world, as babies often do.

Dr. Anne scooped me up and handed me back to my smiling father.

"It's a boy," she said.

Happy birthday to me!

78

James Watson and Dr. Anne were ill-equipped for parenthood, as all new parents are.

If my present-day "self" had any incurable phobias or lingering quirks that were fostered and fed in those earliest days, I am as ignorant to their triggers as you would be to yours. The question of nature vs. nurture takes on even more complex dimensions when the child in question is a genetic clone of his father. If I looked closely enough, I could probably see my entire future, every rotten decision I'm ever going to make, already unfurled in front of me like a rug covered in his muddy footprints. And yet, most times, I've been powerless avoid them. I cannot change who I am; this is a truth I will eventually have to confront. It is like driving the car and being a passenger all at the same time. It's like being in a room inside a room inside a room even bigger than that. Infinite rooms, nested in one another. Impossible.

79

Of course, the INFINITE and IMPOSSIBLE were the only options left for us few and final survivors as we hid from The Gray Tide inside the Motherlove Building downtown.

By this point we had already exchanged all of our worried glances. We had raised our nervous eyebrows and let out our protracted and acquiescent sighs. Today is the day the world ends.

The east wall of the building has collapsed. First, we heard it, sounding not like thunder or a lion's roar, but more like a trillion open mouths chewing on a trillion crunchy tortilla chips. Then, we saw it moving like a fungus, creeping across the building quicker than spilled wine. The mortar melted away.

Still, we did what we could. We did what we could because what else could we do? We cobbled together a second, smaller Even More Impossible Room™ within The Original Impossible Room™, following the new design specs Einar Kjølaas had haphazardly drafted.

(NOTE: Mr. Kjølaas also insisted I started using the trademark symbol (™) when referring The Impossible Room™ and its ancillary chambers from now on. I have done so in the previous paragraph – and in this paragraph too– to appease him, as he was looking over my shoulder just moments ago. But now, satisfied, he has walked away so I am free to say that you, Mr. Kjølaas, can take your tiny ™ symbol and jam it up your ass!)

Where was I?

Oh right. The Even More Impossible Room.

So office furniture was reshaped and repurposed, becoming the unconventional bricks that we stacked up and packed tightly together. It was like assembling a jigsaw puzzle with a blindfold on, to figure out the way all this junk held together.

When we were done an igloo made of folded chairs and twisted desks and broken computer monitors stood before us, a large dome with a small opening in the front for us to crawl through.

I had to work alongside Kelsey, Carol, and my wife Helen. There was no one else left to outsource the labor to, and time was not to be wasted. So I swallowed my pride, and grunted and toiled with the rest of the rabble – all of this work performed under the scornful eye of our de facto pharaoh, the half-Norwegian architect watching over us, saying things like:

"Use these wastepaper baskets to prop up that desk."

—and—

"Set those fax machines on *top* of the filing cabinets."

—and—

"NO, NO, NO DON'T PUT THAT PRINTER THERE, YOU STUPID ASSHOLE. OPEN YOUR STUPID FUCKING EARS AND DO WHAT I TELL YOU."

As you could imagine, as the First and Final King of Motherlove Incorporated, I was not used to being talked to in such a disrespectful manner. My most loyal subjects would never dare. I could not let this insolence stand! And so I said "Now see here, Mr. Kjølaas…"

But before I could finish my sentence, he whipped me with a branch he had torn off a plastic potted tree.

"Silence!" he said.

"But…"

"Build!" he whipped me again and again. "Build! Build! Build!"

So I got silent.

And I built.

I stuffed wet copy paper between the cracks like concrete and scotch taped stationary together into scaffolding. The building we were in was rapidly dissolving. If we just stood here like statues we were going to dissolve too. So I let him whip me and I worked as quickly as I could.

The Tide made the whole Motherlove Building jolt as it ate through a support beam that ran along the east corner. The entire skyscraper leaned to the left, tilted at a 30° angle, like a mountain slope. Pencils and pens rolled across the floor. Landline telephones. Loose change. Tables and chairs, too. Even our second Impossible (Impossibler?) Room shifted and slid on the now-inclined floor, almost collapsing in on itself before it was even finished. The now-askew opening was just wide enough to fit the width of Carol's hips.

Down at the far end of the office, another wall fell away. The Gray Tide swallowed it up in an instant like *crunch crunch crunch* and the Motherlove Building yawned wide open, like there was never a wall there at all.

And below us: there was no more street, no more cars, no more people. There was no more city, state, country or world. There was nothing but The Gray Tide, the sentient ocean, a hungry ball, spread out indefinitely, eating everything. So many mouths that needed to feed. So many hearts beating, desperate, starving, scared. So many monsters, genetically identical to me in every single way. My little brothers, yes.

With the illusionary façade of The Impossible Room now torn away, with the walls gone, we were forced to face a far more upsetting truth, one that had always been but was now unable to be ignored: that this room was never infinite in the first place, and outside had been right there, all along.

80

I was told I cried a lot when I was an infant.

I still cry a lot now as a grown man.

I was crying for the first two days of my life. I lay in my crib, wailing at the top of my lungs. The sky went blue like a bruise as the sun fell away behind the distant hills. The night came. Then the day again. Then the night again. And still I wailed.

By the third morning, my parents couldn't stand it anymore and had taken me to the doctor's office on the far side of town.

My father sat in a familiar chair across from a familiar desk. His sleep-deprived eyes darted around. Yes, he had seen this room before, as well as the grimaced, white-mustached face that stared back at them and their screaming child.

Dr. Caterwaul harrumphed. Still, I cried. He reached down into this desk drawer and rummaged noisily about, before pulling out a roll of scotch tape. He then stood up, walked over to me, and violently wrapped the tape around my head and mouth a half-dozen times, muffling my screams. He walked back behind his desk and sat down.

"There," he said. "Now we can have a conversation like CIVILIZED people."

"So what's wrong with him, doctor?" James Watson asked the medicine man. "Is he...defective?"

"Yes, most likely," Dr. Caterwaul replied. "You have to understand, this child's entire existence is unnatural. You've done a horrible, disgusting, ungodly thing here, Mr. Watson.

If the home owners association knew exactly what you were up to, they'd probably rally with pitchforks and torches and run you out of town. Actually…now that I think about it, that would make a brilliant final scene, don'tcha think? Harkening back to Shelley's *Frankenstein*? We are exploring some similar themes here, albeit in a far stranger and more abstract way."

"Do you think maybe he's hungry?" suggested Dr. Anne.

"Do we have any more Jell-O?" my father said.

"Babies don't eat Jell-O," said Dr. Caterwaul. "They drink milk. From their mothers."

"But I'm his mother," my father said. "And I can't produce milk."

"See? This is exactly what I was talking about," said the doctor. "In my medical opinion, if I were you, I'd put this human larva in a basket and send it down the river. Oh man, can you picture a scene like *that*? The two tearful parents, forced to make the ultimate sacrifice. Is it an act of mercy, or is an act born out of their own selfish desires? Are you monsters yourselves or does your benevolence know no bounds? There's so much gray area we can explore before the rushing waters come and take this child away, his screams fading into the din of the babbling brook, until he is gone, a memory, swept up by the river of time…"

And, as if almost on cue, *tick tick tick* went the clock on the wall. My father looked up at it and saw that the plastic was melting, running down the drywall in heavy, colorful streaks. The minute hand curled up like a blade of burnt grass. The frame of it dissolving like hot wax. Dr. Caterwaul looked confused.

"Are you doing that?" he asked. "How are you doing that?"

"I—I don't know…" my father said. "It's like this poster in my basement. The one by Salvador Dali."

"Hmmm…lotsa intriguing symbolism here," the doctor nodded approvingly, "Now *this* would be a very interesting scene, were it put to film. *This*, my friends, is the very essence of great drama."

81

I eventually stopped crying though.

Not because of anything my parents said or did, but because, inevitably, I ran out of tears.

The same thing happened to a terminally ill James Watson, before my conception took place. He screamed at the sky, until he could scream no longer.

This is one of the secrets of how the world works. In the moment, it all seems so dire. And then everything just...kind of moves on.

82

Here is my first memory:

I'm three year's old. I'm newly mobile. My legs are gangly and awkward, swinging like pendulums. Like I was drunk. I have only a half-dozen younger brothers at this point, not even enough to fill up an egg carton.

My father rarely left the basement. He took his meals down there, slept alone on a soiled mattress, used a bucket for the bathroom, gave birth to his children in a manner that left the area around him looking more like a torture chamber than an operating theater—all of this transpiring down a simple staircase, just below the surface of the street. If you were the mailman, pushing some letters through the slot in the door, you would never even know what was happening beneath you.

Anyway, Dr. Anne was busy trying to wrangle my brothers. At this point she had taken on the role of a nanny and housekeeper, operating (even more than she had been) as an extension of my father's will than of her own volition. Of course, it was her choice to do as such, so maybe it was of her volition. The things we do for love.

The babies she was taking care of were pissing in their diapers and throwing up on themselves and flinging food around the kitchen. Nobody was paying any attention to me.

I wandered through the living room, down the hallway, to the stairs to the second floor. They looked like a mountain, they were so tall. Mount Everest, here in my home. Everything is daunting, when you're little.

But I started to climb anyway. Because I didn't know any better. And because I had never been up there before.

I eventually reached the top; a difficult journey for a three year old, sure, but I mention it not to celebrate the simple triumph of a toddler, because once I got up there, in the long and cavernous hall, I began opening doors one-by-one.

Opened a door. An unlit empty room.

Another door. The same. Unadorned ivory walls and an ivory carpet and nothing else.

I opened a third door. The floor, walls, and ceiling, were all entirely made of human skin.

I should've been horrified, but I was not. I was so young, I didn't know yet that rooms were not supposed to be made of human skin. So I walked in. It pulsated all around me, blue veins branching out in every directions like country roads on a soiled map. There was hair growing out of it in wispy patches. And the heat it radiated was clammy and moist, like I was standing in a pneumonia-wet lung. The room was alive. And as I stepped in further, all 6 sides seemed to close in around me. Quivering and pink, the door disappeared beneath the cascading folds of creeping flesh. I had no concept of up or down or left or right anymore. I was lost in it.

I panicked. I screamed. I screamed out "Daddy, daddy, daddy!" but my father was too far away to hear me or help me.

The skin flexed out like there were things beneath it, pressing at it from the inside, something more than tissue and blood. And then a hand landed on my shoulder.

I yelped and whipped around and there was Dr. Anne, scooping me up in her arms.

"Jimmy, what are you doing up here?" she said.

The walls had retracted when she came in. They had responded to her footsteps the way an unruly child might respond to being caught doing something they shouldn't. The way I was responding now.

"This is the skin room," she said. "We don't go in the skin room without supervision."

"But...why skin room?" I said in broken baby English.

"Because, Jimmy, sometimes you need more skin," she said. "Sometimes your body just isn't big enough."

83

And James Watson's body wasn't big enough.

On the worktable were petri dishes. Lined up and labeled, looking like plastic crop circles when viewed from above.

In each petri dish there wiggled another zygote, another clone, partially through development.

"Meet your new batch of brothers," my father said to me, waving his hand over the dishes like a magician calling your attention to his next trick. I was eight years old in this moment. The patter of naked feet on the floor above us. My brothers running around. It sounded like raindrops on tin. It sounded like a stampede.

"Why do you grow them like little beans?" I asked.

"Is this how beans are grown?" he said to me.

"I dunno," I replied.

"Maybe babies and beans aren't all that different. Maybe I've just built a better baby. Maybe I've found a way to streamline the human race."

As he said this to me, and as we looked at my test tube siblings, he was already swollen up with more children. They sat in amniotic sacs beneath his skin, crammed into places where life shouldn't flourish, where people shouldn't fit. His skin—tawny and patchworked, on the verge of necrosis, pulled from the monstrous room on the second floor and hastily grafted onto his body—was pushed out as far as it could be pushed as he struggled to fit his newest litter.

This process had been repeated, again and again, since the day I was expunged from his womb, on the hot pavement of a dead end street, in the suburb of a nameless city.

84

Let's skip ahead a little bit more. All you have to do is blink.

blink

And now I'm fourteen years old, with armpit hair and an angular jaw and a voice that's deep and sonorous, on the cusp of becoming a man myself. I was a freshman in high school at the time. I got terrible grades; Cs, Ds, and Fs. I didn't know why. It's not like I wasn't smart enough, it's just that I was... never any good at tests...

Anyway *blink* and here we are, on the last day my father ever left his basement lab.

By this point, James Watson was already a waddling blob of a man – three times as tall and five times as wide as the average person. He was overflowing out of himself. The process of giving birth to child after child had thrown all of his proportions off and instead of worrying about this aberrant humanoid-thing he was mutating into, he just stuck more babies into the gaps.

So now there were parts of his body he dragged behind him: gangly appendages that biologists hadn't given names, sacks of fat encased in flesh, lumps and bumps bunched up on his side, throwing off his already hobbled gait. There was the hunch on his back that had proliferated and swallowed up half of his head, disappearing his neck, immobilizing his spine. There were extra spigots, aside from the intestinal one, dripping and draining various fluids, each one a different color; a rainbow of secretions. There was his eyes, which would drift, loose like marbles in a washing machine, unable to focus on anything in front of them, rendering my father nearly blind, save for the blur of shapes that would pass before him.

And, perhaps most disturbing of all, there was the black spot on his brain, which had now run out of space inside his skull. It dusky tendrils poked out of his ears and crept across the contours of his face before growing up the sides of the screwdriver still in his forehead like the roots of a tree up an iron fencepost.

85

He had left the basement to go to the mailbox to drop off a letter.

It was sunny that day.

And warm.

And my little brothers were running around the yard, screaming and laughing and crying and fighting and playing and doing whatever else it was that unsupervised children do. Dr. Anne was busy, inside, either feeding the youngest of us or preparing to deliver the next batch.

She only served my father these days, in any capacity in which she could, even going so far as to cut off her breasts at one point and gifting them to him.

"To feed the babies," she said to James with a soft smile, the two wobbling mammary glands held in her hands like they were a set of exquisite earrings.

"You didn't have to do this…" he said.

"Nonsense," she replied, using a staple gun to attach the disembodied breasts to the center of his chest in a single-file line. "I became a doctor to help *humanity*, but I became your lover to help *you*."

Nobody had been paying attention to the property over the last few years. The house had dilapidated: paint peeling, shingles loose, windows caked over with grime. The grass had grown long, then gone brown. Mountains of trash piled up at the curb, more than the garbage men could take away in a truck. It ripened and rotted and the stink wafted throughout the cul-de-sac at the end of Sycamore Lane.

"Must be the summer," my father said to himself, looking at the cloudless blue sky. "Or maybe it's the spring."

It was actually October, but that was irrelevant.

He pointed to the sun and gave it a final wink and then he returned to the basement, moving slowly, like a slug.

86

The letter he put in the mailbox, on his last day outside, was to his ex-wife Petra, to whom, after this moment, all attempted correspondence with would forever cease.

It simply read:

I have outgrown you. I have outgrown everyone.

87

In the present:

We had escaped into the 2nd Impossible Room.

In the center of it, the five of us stood: Kelsey, Carol, Einar Kjølaas, my wife Helen, and me. A cubicle panel was use to seal up the exit behind us. There was no way out, and hopefully, no way in.

It was dark in here, of course, save a couple of slivers of pale light leaking in through the cracks between copy machines. Jagged shadows stretched out across the floor.

"That was close," said Carol, her voice barely more that shadow itself.

Even though the igloo of office furniture we had erected and climbed into was only the size of a two-car garage, once inside, the room seemed as big and cavernous as an empty airplane hangar; when we walked our footsteps echoed like thunder, and when exhaled our breath roared out of our lungs like waterfalls.

Beyond that: the faint sound of The Grey Tide eating everything outside of these hastily-erected walls could be heard. Our makeshift sanctuary rattled and shook. The Motherlove Building must surely be gone at this point, The Tide surrounding us on all sides. This room is all that is left, suspended inside the thick of it.

Einar Kjølaas lit up another cigarette. The tip glowed orange and we could see each other's faces a little more clearly.

Worried visages, all around, almost indistinguishable, except for one. He inhaled and the firelight flared up, making his features deeper, more pronounced. Smoke curled around his head. And the architect smiled.

"So what are we supposed to do now?" asked Kelsey.

"What to do, what to do…" Einar Kjølaas repeated, as if he were singing the chorus to a song. "Well…Kelsey, is it?… well Kelsey, all we have to do is take apart the walls we're in, disassemble them from the inside out, while refashioning them around us, again. A third room, inside the second room, even smaller and even more impossible."

"Hold on. Stop. This doesn't make any sense!" I said. "This isn't a solution. It defies physics. It defines conceptualization. This is madness!"

Einar Kjølaas breathed out slowly, exasperatedly, as he pulled the thin cigarette from between his lips, rolling the filter between his two fingers before stabbing the lit end into my forearm. I yelped as my skin sizzled and the butt went out. He then kicked me in the shin and I involuntarily dropped to my knees in front of him.

"For a dead man you ask a lot of questions, you know that?" he said.

He then grabbed my wife Helen by her waist and kissed her on the mouth. She didn't fight him. In fact, she embraced him. Kissed him back. She moaned in pleasure. Their white, dehydrated tongues finding their way into each other's mouths.

Just like that, I was no longer King of Motherlove.

No longer the King of the Earth.

I was no one.

88

And so we build ourselves another Impossible Room, inside of the one we were in.

And we climbed inside of it, in a single-file. We entered another rickety dome of infinite space, just as the walls outside it crumbled apart. It was a harrowing and frenzied escape, just like the last time, and I would describe to you in rich and expressive detail, except soon after that we had to do it again for a fourth time.

Then again, for a fifth.

Each time we entered a new room it was smaller than the last. And yet, when we were inside of it, it seemed as endless as the first. We could filter soccer stadiums into this place. We could set up some desks and chairs and reopen Motherlove and everything could return to normal.

Except The Tide kept coming. Following us.

A sixth time. A seventh.

Eighth. Ninth. And tenth.

Our rooms shrinking as we built them, it was part of the design, copying the blueprints over and over, utilizing less and less materials. We went from a hangar to a garage to a coffin to a shoebox. Then to a pillbox. A microchip. Smaller and smaller and smaller still.

Until we were as small as we could get. We were subatomic, I suppose. Or maybe we were even smaller than that. I had nothing to help gauge our size. And there was no more material left to build from. And while the room we were in appeared to be impossibly large, we all knew the simple and impending truth:

This was the end of the line.

89

I do not know what will happen to us, now that there's nowhere left to go. But I will tell you what happened to James Watson, after he took that final trip outside:

He retreated back to the basement, to birth more babies into the world, and when he needed more skin to fit them all in, Dr. Anne went to the 'skin room' and cut some off the wall. She attached it to his body as simply as if she were stitching and sewing two pieces of fabric together. As if she were making a quilt.

There were other rooms upstairs too. The 'bone room' where ribs and femurs sprouted from the wood like saplings, or the 'blood room' full of sanguine puddles dug into the floor, or the 'organ room' packed tight with spleens and livers and bladders and pituitary glands, growing up the wallpaper like grapes on a vine.

They created these biological rooms using the same technology my father had used to clone himself. It wasn't even all that complicated, at least not in comparison to cloning yourself and carrying it to term. You could have 'skin rooms' in your house, if you so desired.

So Dr. Anne would harvest what she needed from the second floor and bring it down to him. She would chainsaw an ulna loose, ladle out a jug of crimson plasma, pluck a gallbladder from its stalk and stick it in her pocket for later.

James Watson continued expand his physical space, growing

larger and larger, until he took up almost all of the basement, bloated like a water balloon filled up too full, his frame pressing up against all four corners of the back wall, taking the shape of the room itself.

90

And I know what you're thinking:

Why didn't my father just grow his babies in jars? They were conceived in test tubes, why not leave them there until they were done? Why didn't he fill up fish tanks with fetuses and go on with his day? Why didn't he dig a hole in the backyard and build himself an Olympic-sized womb?

Why force all of these nascent, half-formed, half-people into his body?

Why suffer?

Well…unless you've ever impregnated yourself with your own clone(s), how could you POSSIBLY know what it feels like? Most people live their whole lives at one miserable speed. James Watson did too, for way longer than he would've liked, until the day he began gestating me.

And look:

Maybe this was just an insane and feverish attempt at correcting all his former mistakes, like some kind of self-flagellating type penance. Or maybe this was brought on by the existential terror that can only come when you've been diagnosed with a black spot on the brain. Who knows! Whatever the case may be, the end result was the same: this was a responsibility that he wanted to take on. So what else could he do but follow through to the best of his ability? We're all searching for a purpose, even if we don't understand it.

91

And so he kept growing.

And soon he couldn't fit in the basement anymore either.

Dr. Anne took an axe and smashed apart the kitchen floor, and the living room floor too, so that my father's body could swell up through them. Like magma from the deep, he rose up in bubbles of goose-dimpled flesh, human putty, remolding itself to its current barriers.

And not long after that, Dr. Anne didn't even have to continue transplanting the bones and blood from upstairs anymore either. Parts of James Watson grew through the structure of the house itself, and those rooms just became a part of him. When he needed more bones, they would migrate under the fleshy floorboards, honed like monarch butterflies heading south, before embedding themselves wherever they were needed to further prop himself up and press himself out. When he needed more blood, veins like cray-zee straws would dangle down from the ceiling and slurp it up. Seven strategically-placed hearts kept the plasma pumping through the walls.

His face grew like a pimple on top of the bloated mass, in the den, where the television would've gone had we a television to put there. It was large, almost the size of a garage door, stretched out and distorted, a crooked smile that spread from the kitchen to the hall.

"Hello honey," he said to Dr. Anne through his mutant lips.

"Hello lover," she replied.

92

And Dr. Anne.

Poor, beleaguered Dr. Anne.

Things were not going to end well for her.

And I'm sure some of you are reading this paragraph right now going: wait a minute here, Jimmy Watson Jr., surely Dr. Anne deserved more—both as a human being with autonomy, and as a character in this rambling narrative—than to play the innocent Igor to my father's Victor Frankenstein!

And to that I say: yes, she certainly *did* deserve more. Motherfucker, that's my POINT. Don't we all?

But to call her innocent? That, my friend, she was not.

I told you she was selfless.

I told you she was in love.

That can be a lethal combination, if you're not careful. And if the world were just, perhaps Dr. Anne would get her own book. Of course, if the world were just there would still be a world.

She gave more and more of herself to my father. Both emotionally and physically, because that's what he needed and that's what she had to give. He took it all: breasts, belly, legs, arms, and brains. Absorbing them into his body, making them a part of him. All of her, until one day, without much fanfare, he had consumed her completely and she was just…

….gone.

93

Meanwhile, under his flesh, things were flourishing still:

He had fetuses tucked between folds of muscle, filed behind organs, crammed into whatever pockets of meat he was able to spare. Intestinal tubes like sewage pipes passed in and out of his body, crisscrossed around the room like exposed pipes, dripping with mucus and shit. Inside the intestines, you could hear them, my unborn brothers, scurrying around my father's body like tiny hamsters.

He had gestation down to only two weeks, and he could carry to term five dozen babies at a time. An entire litter; a veritable zoo. Over and over and over again, the babies getting smaller and the pregnancies getting more efficient with every pass. And he was still working on his formulas, still writing in his notebook, still refining the process of cloning himself.

They came out of him the size of a quarters, leaking from a vaginal slit he had Dr. Anne insert underneath his chin. He wouldn't even go into labor anymore; he would just clear his throat and tilt his head back and five dozen infants would come slithering out of his neck and into the world. Each time Dr. Anne's arms would appear like she too was under my father's skin. Out of the fat they would form, malnourished but ever-matronly, and help guide the child into the world.

Five dozen more perfect copies of him.

Five dozen more perfect copies of me.

94

This process continued, unabated and unchecked, until my father summoned me one afternoon.

"Son No. 1," he said. His voice was little more than a vibration that carried itself throughout the framework of the house. His words rattled the foundation, rattled his bones. Everything creaked and crawed. You could feel his voice settling inside you, deeper than your own thoughts.

It was uncommon for him to be speaking at all these days. Even less common for him to be speaking directly to me, even though he was physically woven into the building I lived in.

"Most houses don't talk," he explained to me once, corpulent floor quivering beneath my feet. "Most walls tell no stories. Most walls are just walls."

95

That is to say, he had done his best to be a house:

The speed and frequency at which James Watson had been replicating himself required a massive amount of energy, and so most of the time he just sat there, inert, trying to conserve his strength; sewn in to the structures that kept the building from collapsing in on itself. From the outside, my father was a normal house to behold.

That was why:

The power lines that ran up and down the street were plugged directly into his sides. He sucked electricity from the grid like a thirsty child sucked down soda pop. And still, even as he hummed and whirred, he demanded more and more. He always need more. We couldn't run the microwave and the hairdryer at the same time or a fuse would blow. Every time he inhaled, the streetlights in the neighborhood dimmed.

Still:

Inside of him, my younger brothers did most of the grunt work. They served him in all the ways he couldn't serve himself, working in his basement, inside his bowels, mixing together the concoctions and chemicals that would make more of him. More of themselves. The formula had been tweaked even more by then. My brothers weren't growing to the size of your average human, nor had they the same kind of thoughts and desires that most people define themselves by. They were the size of field mice, reaching full maturation in only a few days, and they worked incessantly. They were industrious and focused, feeding on glucose taps they had installed into James Watson's liver, sleeping in whatever meat folds they could find. Their skin was almost clear, pale and unhealthy, taking on a silver pallor.

They didn't question my father's motives. They knew their place in these big, ugly cosmos; to be a part of this human machine and carry out its duties, whatever they may be. My father gave them a purpose which they gladly accepted.

And yet:

I tell you now, as I told him on that day…I've never felt that way.

I was his son too. That assuredness should've also been mine!

But here I am. I've never felt truly happy. I've never felt truly loved. I've never felt content. I too have always wanted more. This was the narrative loop that played over in my head, again and again, the sound of the only drum I could march to. And now I stood, at 18 years old, a man myself, genetically similar to this house I lived in, blindly facing the inescapable future in which I was doomed, watching all my brothers around me seemed to fall so comfortably into place.

And so when I asked him:

"What is wrong with me? Why am I the broken one?"

He told me:

"We are all born broken. It's part of the design."

96

And if Dr. Caterwaul were around at that moment to blast my head with x-ray beams, he would hold up the transparencies for me now and point to the black spot in my skull and say:

"You and him have the same black spot in the same sick brain. You can't avoid it, Jimmy!"

And my father knew this day would eventually come. And when that same dark diagnosis was bequeath onto me, James Watson, the human house, spoke —and the floorboards shuddered and the drainpipes roared— and he said:

"This was why I worked so hard, why I couldn't be there for you in the way a father perhaps should, why I consumed Dr. Anne, why I consumed our home and everyone in it, why I had to grow so big – much bigger than any one person has a right to be. Doing this to myself was the only way I knew how to tell you I loved you."

97

"But I don't understand where I fit into this," I said my father. "I don't even understand who or what am I? Where I belong?"

"You were my first," he said, "Mistakes were made, as any beginner can attest. Mistakes I have since corrected over time."

A herd of my little mouse-sized brothers ran past my feet, carrying partially-constructed organs from one chamber of my father's body to another. The room was pink and corpulent, like the lining of an esophagus, and it trembled around me as James Watson breathed.

His face took up the entire living room, and I stood in the middle of it. One of his jackfruit-shaped eyes had moved upward, so that it hung from above like a chandelier. The other eye was the size of a satellite dish, bloodshot and heavy. His lipless mouth like a canyon, tongue lolling about in the gap. And, amidst the chaos of his disfigured parts, was a tiny half-melted screwdriver, still sticking out of what once was his forehead. Thick black lines extended out from it, far beyond the brain in which they originally found purchase, to fill up external space around us. Above and below and on all sides, the black spot besieged the room. Tentacles lain wet like tar and throbbing as they continued to crawl along the floor, around my sneakers, towards the front door.

"I wanted to protect you," he said.

"Protect me…from what?"

"From the world. From the future. From everything."

"But I'm a mistake. You said it yourself," I said. "I'm not like my brothers; smaller parts of a whole. I'm unnatural. An oddity. I shouldn't exist."

"You're right," he said. "But tell me, Jimmy, what *should* exist, either natural or not? By any metric one could measure such things, life on Earth is improbable at best. And yet here we are, me and you and everyone else. It's a miracle. But it's a miracle that comes with a price. Every day, when all the work is done, we must reconcile the knowledge that it is all temporary. That death is certain. That death is forever. And as hard as I tried, I could not save you and your brothers from that.

"BUT I did the next best thing, son: I improved the formula, as you can see. I removed their self-doubt. I gave them all a purpose. To make more of themselves. More of us. It's as lofty an objective as any.

"And maybe it is just an artifice, in the end. A slight-of-hand I've pulled to shield them from their unavoidable fate. But so what? With no questions, there is no fear. That seems like a gift to me.

"My greatest regret is that I wasn't able to do that for you, Jimmy, when Dr. Anne and I were still incompetent new parents. I didn't know how yet. I didn't know anything. But time moved forward, as time does, and I was able to rewrite the rules. You and me, we are the same. Genetically. And it's not too late for you to be happy…"

But I thought:

If we were the same, as he claimed, then he must know how I felt:

He must know that my blood felt poisonous.

He must know that the same black spot polluted me as it polluted him. The dark tendrils that spread out across the floor rose up and slammed back down, forever restless, forever discontent.

He must know that I wanted to cry, because what else was one supposed to do at a moment like this but cry?

But before I could contextualize and process any of these thoughts (as I have the benefit of doing now) I felt a pall suddenly come over the room. It was almost instinctive, like I had just stepped into the shadow of a predator. Something was wrong.

The light from the windows dimmed. I turned around to see scabs forming over the glass like the rust on a tin can. Brown and flakey. It sounded like tinfoil as the room went red.

"What is happening?" I said.

My father replied: "I can still fix you, Jimmy."

And he said: "I can give you a purpose, too."

And he said: "I built your brothers to be small. To fit inside of me and populate me like a city. I wanted us to all work together as one cohesive unit, one singular mind headed towards a singular goal. But you, Jimmy…you grew into a full-sized person…"

And since my father and I share the same sick pathology, when he said: "I cannot let you leave," I completely understood where he was coming from, because the alternative –an uncertain future in which we all perish– was even more terrifying than that.

His black spot now wrapped around my legs like manacles. "I need all the help I can get. I'm still going to die one day, Jimmy. And how am I supposed to save you when I still haven't even saved myself?"

98

He told me we could make this easy.

"Just surrender yourself," he said. "It'll be just like falling asleep. And when you wake up, you'll just be a part of me again, like you were when you were a baby. We will work together, Jimmy, from the inside. One big family: me, you, Dr. Anne, your brothers. You will share my purpose, and any fear will be divided up amongst many minds; just a tiny, little pocket of fear for each of us, completely manageable. Then all of your concerns can just fade away..."

And he added:

"...or, if that doesn't work for you, we can do this the hard way..."

And the black spot around my ankles grew tighter. Moving up my legs to my waist. I thrashed a little bit, but couldn't move. I looked towards the front door, which disappeared as the black spot crept across handle and jamb. The house was holding me hostage.

"You can't do this," I said.

"Are you telling me what I can and can't do with my body?" he chuckled.

"I'm not a part of you," I said. "I am my own person."

"Yes...yes...yes..." he said. "We still all are our own people, isn't that right, darling?"

The featureless shape of Dr. Anne formed underneath his skin, pressing against it like she was trapped under a sheet.

"It's okay, Jimmy," she said, her voice muffled beneath the

layer of flesh that covered her mouth. She looked like Silly Putty and sounded like she was underwater. "You can trust me."

I tried to run, but couldn't move. Any resistance I offered was returned with equal force. Black tentacles held onto me like I was the only anchor they could find.

"She loved me, Jimmy," my father said. "What greater sacrifice can you think of than giving up your own body for the greater good? She willfully let me assimilate her…because I needed more flesh, more bones, and more blood. She let me take it all from her."

My father was growing impatient with me. The more he tried explaining himself, the more sinister his voice became. The windows and door were completely gone now. I was inside of him with no way to get out, the room illuminated by the amniotic glow of a sickly sun passing through wet flesh. This wasn't just a metaphor, I had returned to the womb.

"You know, Jimmy, you wouldn't be here if it wasn't for me."

"I didn't ask for this."

"None of us did." He exhaled, and now the house shuddered like a growling animal. "Do you know where the cells came from, the ones that I originally cloned you from? Because they weren't from my brain, and they weren't from my heart…"

"From where then?" I asked.

"From the bottom of my foot, Jimmy. I created you from skin flakes from the bottom of my foot."

99

So I said:

"Okay."

"Okay?" he replied.

"Okay. I will join you, father. I will surrender myself into you."

"Jimmy, Jimmy, you've got this all wrong. It's not so much a surrender as it is the next step in your evolution. You were a human foot that learned how to feel, that learned how to think. A foot that knew exactly what it was. This is admirable, for a foot, but we together have so much more work to do! We have to repopulate the whole world. We have to reach as far and as wide as we can. Look at the universe, and the way it expands. That is us, a microcosm.

"You're just one of billions of cells in my body. Just because you can think, it doesn't make you more special than the others. You are making the right choice, my son. For yourself. For us all."

The black spot now coiled around me like a boa constrictor, pinning my arms to my sides and attaching my feet to the ground, twisting and twisting, all the way up to my neck.

I closed my eyes.

Tilted my head back.

Took a deep breath.

And let the tentacle tip of my father's black spot enter my mouth.

100

I disappeared.

poof

(that's the sound you make when you disappear, in case you were wondering)

Just like that I was dead.

But I was only dead for a moment. Like an old computer, I was about to reboot. I was switched off and there was darkness. Nothingness. Or not nothingness exactly, but rather, there was the *absence* of nothingness. Nothingness 2.0: the kind of death you can only achieve if you were never born in the first place. It didn't make any sense, how unimaginably vast this nothingness was.

And then *poof again* there I was. Turned back on.

But I wasn't me. Not entirely, anymore. I still had my body –still sausaged in the same skin I had always known, same prints on the tips of my fingers, same feet I would use to tap my toes– but I was now inexorably a part of my father, physically, mentally, spiritually, wholly. I was more than just his son. That delineation had melted away in the darkness. We were one.

The thing was, I had always known the reasons why my father acted as he did, even before the assimilation. I didn't need to plug myself into this human house to understand it. That same desperation was the reason things were going play out (on an even grander scale, to an even more disastrous end) when I am forced to confront the same existential dilemmas that he faced here.

But in that moment, I did learn something new. As his black spot worked its way through my anatomy, thicker than my own blood, I could finally see his ultimate goal, his endgame, if you could call it that, because what I saw was this:

There was NO goal.

And there was NO endgame.

The transformation he had been going through was the goal unto itself. To grow and change and change the world alike. He only wished to reproduce and expand, continuously, taking over more and more, until there was nothing left.

"The universe is chaos," he said to me, "and we're left to try and derive our own meaning from a set of meaningless circumstances. Some people may call this attitude nihilistic, but I call it hopeful. My plan is as valid for the future as that of any married couple wishing to build a life and have a child together. I couldn't be more human."

Valid? Sure. I could concede to that. Proliferation and propagation is the natural objective of any species, big and small. But as far as species go we were no longer behaving like men.

We were acting more like…a disease.

101

I could sense Dr. Anne in here too.

She appeared to me as a ghost. But she wasn't like the ghosts in spooky Halloween tales. Her specter didn't materialize in front of me, her floating corpse like cigarette smoke, transparent and eyeless. She took no form because *real* ghosts don't have to rely on such cheap gimmicks. Real ghosts haunt you from the inside of your own head. Like an idea. A memory. Your memories are ghosts.

"Dr. Anne?" I said. "Mom, are you there?"

"Jimmy? What are you doing in here?" she said.

We weren't speaking out loud. My father couldn't hear us even though his black spot moved through me, the tips of it smaller and smaller, through my veins, nested in my capillaries.

"I am a monster," I said. "The black spot fills me up too. I was born with it. What else am I supposed to do?"

"I am not an angel," she said. "I didn't come to save you, or assist you, or give you a purpose. I lost myself as willfully as any other foolish explorer treading across the unmapped areas of the human heart."

"Was it the right choice?" I asked.

Dr. Anne chuckled and said:

"How the hell am I supposed to know?"

102

"It's too late for me," I said to her. "I've already let him inside me, and now I am stuck inside him. I must resign myself to that."

"If that's what you want, then so be it," Dr. Anne said to me in the dim-lit dungeon of my father's bowels. "But these walls are your walls now too, Jimmy. The same blood flows through you. If you want the door open, all you need to do is open it."

103

Turns out, she was right. It really was that easy.

All I had to do was think about opening the front door and the front door reappeared.

I suppose Dr. Anne could've done the same, if she had wanted to; reassemble herself the same way she gave herself up –piece by piece– and move on with her life. Then again, we're all capable of way more than we ever end up accomplishing, so who even knows.

"What are you doing? Where do you think you are you going?" James Watson bellowed as the flesh receded like a stage curtain at the start of a play. It opened up like dilated labia, revealing a passageway out of his body. The daylight from outside beckoned, golden freedom.

"You can't do this," he said.

"I have to," I replied.

"Get back here, Jimmy. Get back here. GET BACK HERE!"

He screamed and screamed, but I didn't respond. Instead, I concentrated even harder, reaching inwardly with my mind, and forced my father's black spot to uncoil from the folds of my muscles and bones. And when it was done and I was released, I brushed off my shoulders and headed for the exit.

My little brothers tried to stop me from leaving. Why wouldn't they? They knew no other life than this. At least fifty of them rushed up and surrounded my feet, attempting to hold me in place, but I effortlessly waded through them as if I were wading through a puddle of mud. A little gray puddle of mud…

And so:

I left my father's house, passing through membranes and sinew and dangling corpuscles like we were in an abattoir. Slime and mucus covering my ragged frame, pink and new, down the canal, towards the light.

I stepped though.

And I was reborn.

104

Of course being reborn was nothing like being born the first time.

Nobody consults the infant before wrenching it out of the infinite and impossible darkness. We all begin the exact same way. We scream our way out of the void. It's part of what unites us all as human beings.

But my rebirth was my choice. How many people get to consciously make such an important decision? To say *yes please, I* would *like to face the terror of the unknown, thank you for asking.* This time I entered the world with no trauma, no cataclysm, no tears. This time, it was sublime. The sun beat down on my skin and the air filled up my lungs and I had my entire life still left to live, and every choice was lain out in front of me like tomatoes at an endless salad bar.

My name was Jimmy Watson Jr. and I was just getting started.

cue the inspirational music

104 (again)

Except there was one thing I failed to mention.

Before I walked out of James Watson's new-formed vaginal door –heels clicking against the fleshy floor and elbows pointed confidently towards the sky– I spotted something that caused me to pause.

On a janky pile of unnamable bones (his anatomical attempt at emulating an end table, I'm guessing?) my father's notebook sat. You know the notebook I'm referring to, right? I've mentioned it several times in this book before. Perhaps I should've been writing it in all capital letters, to illustrate its importance. If there was ever a comprehensive mythology written about my father (perhaps that is what I have been writing?) then The Notebook would surely be as fundamental to it as the Ten Commandments, etched in stone and irrevocable.

THIS was The Notebook where he jotted down his ideas.

THIS was The Notebook where he kept all his formulas.

Since the very beginning –well before I was ever conceived– until that very afternoon, on that very day: THIS is where all the important information concerning me and my brothers' design and creation was archived and logged. Mathematically, biologically, philosophically, The Notebook was the Rosetta Stone, the skeleton key.

So did I betray my father by stealing it from him as I hastily made my escape?

Perhaps.

And I couldn't tell you exactly why I did, other than that I could feel in me the same selfish and desperate desires that drove him here in the first place. I wanted my life to mean something. I wanted answers. I wanted to prove, to myself and to everyone else, that I was here, that I existed, and that I mattered.

So I snatched up The Notebook as I ran out the door and down the street, with the intention of never returning again.

cue the ominous music that signifies that I, like my father before me, will too be a victim of my own hubris

105

The next ten years my life played out in almost the exact same way my father's had, except I had an arsenal of knowledge and insight he did not, gleaned from The Notebook and my experience as his first-born son. So then, where he failed, I was able to succeed. It was the funhouse mirror inversion of his shitty life as I retraced the same steps he had took that lead him the point where this narrative began:

I got a job a Motherlove Incorporated.

In the Paint Division. Just like him.

But that was just to get my foot in the door. I had greater aspirations than watching paint dry.

I used The Notebook and my father's formulas to quickly leverage myself up the corporate ladder, even though I (like James) had no formal schooling or technical training. But I passed his math and science off as mine, bullshitting whenever I couldn't quickly and clandestinely reference his writings.

"Oh yes," I would say as I lead the other scientists down the white halls of Motherlove's Research and Development Laboratories. "The quadratic equation of the…um…isosceles triangles…are…uh…the square root of…pi."

I met my would-be wife and future queen Helen amongst the twisted catacombs of computer screens and cubicles in The Impossible Room. We married and moved into a house on a street on the opposite side of town from Sycamore Lane. And when the bushy-mustached Dr. Caterwaul sat me down in his office and (unsurprisingly) told me I was sterile, Helen stayed by my side, whereas James Watson's ex-wife Petra did not.

Of course, it wasn't love at first sight between me and Helen. If I'm being honest, it wasn't love at all. But we pretended. And most days, pretending was pretty much as good as the real thing. It was easy to act like we were the characters in a fairy tale, whom serendipity had brought together, and not just two random people who happened to be marginally-attracted to each other within convenient geographical proximity.

All I know is that, years later, when she kissed Einar Kjølaas in front of me while the world ended around us, I felt nothing. No jealousy. No sadness. I did not care. And I thought: maybe James Watson and Dr. Anne had figured out something Helen and I had not. Maybe love is the most sacred and precious commodity of them all.

Or maybe none of this really matters.

And the next time I went to visit Dr. Caterwaul, he showed me an x-ray of the black spot in my skull, confirming what I knew was always going to be in store for me. Death was as certain as the image of my brain he held in his hands. But I was too busy with work, with Helen, with all these distractions to deal with that, so I pushed the existential terror away with equal parts denial and platitude, saying dumb shit like "that's life" and "nobody lives forever". Like acquiescing myself to the truth somehow mitigated it.

But we build upon the past. That's how humankind has always marched forward –how we ended up with rocket ships and skyscrapers and The Impossible Room– facing the darkness by paving over it and calling the world our own, until the day the first Infinitassium tablet was completed.

That changed everything.

I was handed the prototype. The first supplement of its kind, derived from the numbers my father had chicken-scratched in his notebook. The very same numbers that made me.

Infinitassium was the cure to death. I could fit it in my palm: a little gray pill, so small you could swallow it dry, if you desired to.

106

All of these things transpired, more or less, as I sat back and passively shrugged my way through it all. As I whoopsie-daisy'ed my way into the history books. As the world rejoiced, before it fell apart. As it fell apart, and I ascended to king. As my kingdom fell apart, and my time ran out.

107

And so:

Infinitassium in my pocket –a full two months before The Gray Tide rolled in– I sat in the back of a slow-moving taxi cab. It cut its way left and right through the neighborhoods on the outskirts of town, gravel crunching under its tires, engine puttering like a pneumonic old man.

"Long way to go," the taxi driver said.

I looked up and our eyes met in the review mirror.

"I'm sorry, what?" I said.

"The ride. All the way across town."

"Yeah," I said. "I suppose it is."

"Must be a pretty important trip, to go out this far."

"You're kinda nosy for a cab driver."

"Hey, I'm just making conversation, man," he said. "We ain't gotta talk if you don't want to. Most people ride the bus out this way. I never get to see these suburban streets. They're nice."

"I grew up out here," I said.

"Oh yeah? Musta been alright. Safe."

"No," I said. "No, it wasn't safe."

The taxi turned onto Sycamore Lane, and the driver said:

"Sometimes I look at the city, and these suburbs, and all the people in 'em, and it's just too much. Like, I don't even know how we handle it. How we don't just all go crazy. Think about it, my man. This moment –RIGHT NOW– is the pinnacle of all mankind's endeavors, the end result of millions of years of evolution, the sum total of every mind that dared to dream. That's a lot of responsibility put on the shoulders of regular folks like us. We got a lot to live up to."

The breaks squeaked as we pulled up to the curb at the end of the cul-de-sac. A shadow swallowed the car, as if the sun had just been eclipsed. The cab driver's mouth hung open as I stepped out from the backseat and threw a few extra dollars his way.

"What the fuck is that thing?!" he said.

"That's my father," I replied. "I'm home."

108

There wasn't an entranceway to get in or out of him.

He was all swollen up, as incongruous in the cul-de-sac as a mesa upon a prairie, as a blistering volcano that wanted to erupt. Abutting two nearly-identical colonials, he dwarfed the rest of the neighborhood by nearly three stories, a wobbling blob of distorted meat that took up the entire property, yard and all. The house I grew up in had disappeared into him completely, deconstructed and repurposed, inexorably woven throughout his body.

Hair covered the roof in awkward clumps, slicked against his skin shingles with oily sweat. His face had migrated to the center of the mass, assuming the visage of the building they had become: eyes like the picture windows, staring up at the sun like thirsty solar panels, and his mouth sat where a front door might've gone, gnawing at the air with hundreds of crooked teeth in yellow gums. His arms and legs, no longer of use, had receded into his bulk and had been taken apart and reassembled as organs more conducive to maintaining his current state. He was an ecosystem, an entire universe, unto his own, as countless clones worked like tireless prisoners, trapped inside of him, making more of themselves. Making more and more.

And then there was the black spot.

The black spot on his brain.

The black spot on his brain that had grown EVERYWHERE.

The screwdriver that stuck out of his former forehead looked so tiny when protruding from this now house-sized man, yet from the puncture wound thousands of sable tentacles had sprouted. They wrapped themselves all around his frame like the ivy on the bricks of an old college. They got thick at points, wider than tree trunks, and thin at others, as gossamer as spider silk. Not only crossing his body with greater density than his own veins, they spread out across what was left of the yard, the driveway, into the street itself, dug through the pavement and the dirt like a plant, anchoring him into ground. I had to step over and walk around these bulging roots as I made my way up to him.

"Dad?" I said.

"Jimmy?" he replied, though his eyes didn't roll in my direction. I suspect they didn't work at all anymore, at least not in the way that eyes were supposed to.

"What are you?" I said as the scent of him hit me. Death. He smelled like a dead body.

"What...are you...?" he said back. It strained him to speak. His words came out, laborious and slow, but also, as a chorus, as if there were an amphitheater of voices inside of him all whispering the same words he spoke out loud. All of my brothers inside him, all saying the same thing.

"I'm a man," I told him.

"Overrated," he replied.

I dug into my pocket and pulled out the Infinitassium, holding up the gray pill between my thumb and index finger. No more conspicuous than an aspirin.

"This is why I've come here," I said.

"What is...that supposed...to be?"

"We call it Infinitassium."

"Infinit...assium," he echoed me.

"It's a daily dietary supplement," I said. "Like a vitamin. Except it cures you of all disease. It repairs and regenerates all your cells. It make you healthy, makes you stronger. All this... shit you've destroyed yourself over, trying to understand? All these years of self-harm and struggle? The answer to it is right here. It was here the whole time, if only you had…looked. Dad, I invented a pill that has made death obsolete."

He exhaled. Or did the house equivalent of exhaling. I could see ripples move across his skin; clones like termites running through him, thicker than blood. And then he said:

"Why?"

"Why? Why *what*? Why did I cure death?"

"No, why…did you come here?"

I wanted to scream at him:

"Why did I come here? Why? WHY? Because I need VALIDATION, you neglectful fuck! Because I am VAIN, I am PROUD, and I am a NARCISSIST, just like YOU! Because you created me, against my will, and now I want REVENGE!"

But instead I simply said:

"I don't know."

109

And I continued:

"I took your notebook."

"You did what?" he said.

"Your notebook –The Notebook with a capital N– the one full of your formulas. On the day that I left, I took it with me. Swiped it right off the end table."

"Jimmy…"

"So careless you were. So full of arrogance. To just leave it there, to treat like it was no more important than a recipe book, to act like I would be content as just an ingredient in the stew.

"Well I went through it, old man. I read every page. And not only that, but I sold off its contents to Motherlove Incorporated, one piece at a time. And I was rewarded by doing so. I have a wife, a house, a career, a LIFE." I sighed. "All these *things*, they could've been yours, if you hadn't let that black spot take over. You had the answers right there, in your hand. You could've used them any time. You could've WON."

"My first born son…are you so thick…as to not see the whole picture here? Do you not think…that I left that notebook…there on purpose…for you to take…?"

My mouth fell open, thunderstruck, and said: "What?!"

"I wanted you to take The Notebook. I knew…you would. I knew you would…because that's what I would've done. Everything you've done…is what I would've done, were I in the places you were…when I got there. Can you see, now, where you fit into all this? You have always been…a little bee… but I will forever be your hive. You can fly all around….go *buzz buzz buzz*…but in the end…you belong to me. I always knew…one day you'd return. And here…we are."

"You set me up?" I said, trying to understand. "You let me leave?"

"I let you leave so you could go…and get to work…and come back to me…and bring me…that."

He couldn't motion to it, but I knew what he meant. The Infinitassium tablet. The prototype. The first of its kind. In the palm of my hand.

"This is…what we were working towards…this entire time," he said. "And I think you know…what I need you to do…"

And I should've known better. I should've just left. But I didn't.

And maybe, in a way, what I was about to do was an act of forgiveness. Or maybe it was an act of benevolence. Or compassion. Or maybe it was foolishness, or familial duty, or mercy, or confusion. Maybe it was all those things. Maybe I didn't have a choice. Maybe none of us have a choice, ever. Maybe there are no missteps. Maybe there has only ever been one path forward, and life was nothing more than an endless funeral procession along it.

It's not really my place to say.

But what I do know is this:

I walked up to my father, so that I was mere inches from his quivering mass. He was hot, like an oven. I could hear my brothers inside him, the multitude of feet plodding throughout his body, going *thonk* against bone and *squish* against meat, no doubt carrying out further experiments, making more of themselves, taking whatever steps were to come after this.

I reached up and wrapped my hand around the base of the screwdriver sticking out of the center of his former forehead. My father winced as I dug my heels into the soil and pulled with all my might, until it popped out. Tentacles whipped around my head like a hungry squid was descending from above, but before they could wrap themselves around me, before I even let the screwdriver slip from my palm, I had jammed the Infinitassium tablet into the open wound and stepped back.

"Thank you," my father said.

"You're welcome," I replied.

I was inescapably my father's son.

110

The ground shook and the earth quaked as the black spot unmoored itself from the pavement. It rattled the neighborhood at the end of Sycamore Lane. I looked behind me and saw Brad and Jennifer Flatly in their living room, peering out their picture window in terror and awe.

The branches of the black spot curled up, dried out –as brittle and as thin as twigs– before disintegrating completely. The black spot was cast to the air like dust. Dispersed by the breeze. Gone.

My father's body expanded rapidly outward, faster than it ever had before, like a hot air balloon. Or because of his oblong dimensions, he looked more like a blimp.

Like latex his pores had healed over. All the cuts and lacerations that covered his flesh disappeared. He looked shiny, polished, like he had just been taken out of the package, new.

And then, when he stopped talking to me, all his teeth fell out at once, hundreds of them raining down like a struck piñata. His lips melted into each other as if they were made of candle wax. When he went to blink, his eyelids stayed closed. His earholes and nostrils pushed upward and outward, completely sealing up. He wasn't breathing.

Was this an allergic reaction of some sort? I wondered if I should be alerting the Motherlove scientists as to what I was observing here. They were the ones with the clipboards and clicky-pens, who kept and cataloged any possible side-effects:

The subject has taken on balloon-like qualities.

But the scientists weren't here and this wasn't a test and my father wasn't experiencing anaphylaxis at all. Quite the opposite, really. The Infinitassium tablet was working *too well*.

I bet the clones inside him were passing the drug around like a bottle of expensive wine. I bet it was a party that evening inside James Watson's bowels. I bet there were banners thumbtacked to his intestinal walls that read CONGRATS TEAM and MISSION ACCOMPLISHED.

He slowly rose off the ground. When the foundation of the house broke free, blood squirted from the fleshy bricks, filling storm gutters with crimson slime.

Higher he went.

He was a cloud upon a zephyr. My brothers, his clones, reproduced faster and faster than they had before. They sloshed around inside him. They breathed in and out, hundreds of thousands of tiny lungs, filling him up with their hot air. And with the exits sealed and nowhere for those gases to escape, he inflated. The human house became the human zeppelin. It was an otherwise sunny day, but my father eclipsed the sun and cast his odd shadow of the entire city.

He floated up and up before he disappeared to the west, over the horizon.

111

It was a miracle, I had thought.

He had ascended to the heavens.

He sacrificed himself so that the rest of us could live eternally.

He was the big man in the sky.

And in the two months that followed that day:

Infinitassium went into full production. Ads ran on TV and the radio, celebrity spokespeople telling the desperate throngs that there was no reason to be afraid, ever again. The pills were bottled and shipped out to stores, stocked on endcaps with signage full of proclamations and price points: $35.99 for a month's supply. A small price to pay for immortality. You didn't need a prescription.

I even went so far as to tell the Motherlove execs where the formula had come from.

"This more than just my life's work, it was my father's work too. We did this…together."

The CEOs all looked at each other and shrugged, like they could give a shit where the formula had come from. Was it going to be profitable? Then GOOD!

Occasionally, my father would be spotted, floating placidly across the sky. There he was, above Germany, a satellite of bloated meat.

A parade was held in our honor.

My father passed over South Korea. The size of a storm cell, obscuring the light.

They wrote about us in *Time* and the *New Yorker*.

My father, as swollen and as round as the moon, hanging over the Indian Ocean. Speculation and rumors about what he was doing there abounded. Some said he was caught in a gyre of crosswinds, held in place by circulating sea breeze off the Malabar Coast and the rotation of the earth. Others said he just got tired of flying around, and needed to rest.

Whatever the case, he hovered over the Indian Ocean for several weeks, as the Infinitassium tablets were manufactured and distributed. He hovered over the Indian Ocean as the world became immortal. He hovered over the ocean as his body continued to grow, until it could harbor no more weight, until this entire endeavor became too cumbersome to bear, until one day:

Like a meteorite, he came crashing back down to Earth. Into the sea, he plummeted, landing with such force that giant waves washed up and over the nearest beaches. Local trawlers and fishing boats were contracted and dispatched. They combed the water, the endless blue ocean, looking for James Watson's corpse.

And then they found it. No longer puffed up like it was. No longer even full of muscle or bones. He was just empty skin, like a circus tent with no one in it. He stretched out for miles, a blanket on the sea. They pulled him up on a vessel, folding him up and storing him in the cargo hold in the hull. They shipped him back to the city. The James Watson Memorial Garden was constructed in the westernmost corner of Elysium Grounds and we buried him under the monolith inscribed with his name.

And the rest of us lived happily, forever ever after.

112

That would've been a nice ending to this book.

Forever ever after. How cute.

But as you already know, that was not possible.

Even with all the work we've done, with all the experiences we've shared, with all the things we've learned and are learning still, some things were still unavoidable.

Soon after James Watson's deflated husk had been pulled out of the water, the patch of ocean where he crash landed turned a cadaverous shade of gray.

At first, no one could explain it. Some sort of new algal bloom? A change in the barometric pressure causing the light that refracted off the surface to shimmer in a color other than blue? Mass delusional paranoid psychosis triggered by the emotional overload of our newfound immortality?

It was none of those things, though.

It was The Gray Tide.

113

Some may call it a reckoning, an inevitability. I was not a doomsayer back then so I was not fretful myself. Something would work out, I told myself. Something always did.

The force of the impact caused his skin to rupture open. All my tiny brothers spilled out of him. They were released into the sea like the first protozoa on a promising young planet, swimmmmmmmmming away!

Because what happened was this:

By now, all of these impossibly tiny James Watson's working together had figured out how to replicate themselves without gestating at all. But they didn't split in two, as one might suspect, like bacteria in the process of mitosis. This wasn't simple cell division. These little James Watson's had progressively become so small that they were now subatomic; more miniscule than the blocks from which all reality was built. They were the size of elementary particles themselves. From here, my brothers could easily deconstruct solid matter using nothing more than their bare hands. They tore neutrons and protons out of nuclei. They plucked elections out of the air like apples from trees. They made applesauce out of it.

And this microscopic miasma? This molecular stew? All they had to do from here was rearrange those particles in a very precise way and they could reshape the world into whatever they wanted, whether it be a blade of grass or a droplet of rain…

…or a carbon copy of James Watson himself, another mini-version of my father that will repeat this very same process, again and again, until there was nothing left.

Ecophagy was the technical term for what was happening here. Look it up; it's a real word. It literally translates to "the eating of one's own house."

My brothers reproduced exponentially. This was how they managed to spread so widely, so quickly, taking over most of the planet after just a few days. Everything was consumed and conquered.

The media (when there was still a media around) called it The Gray Tide because of its pale color. Gray, like the dead flesh of a once-living man.

And The Tide came rolling in. Evolving out of the water and onto the land, a biological tsunami comprised of trillions upon trillions of individual, sentient beings – in concert as they headed towards their common, apocalyptic goal. Against that many hands, there wasn't much any of us could do.

It stank of death and shit and rot. It wailed like a choir under duress. Picture ants atop a dollop of ice cream –but EVERYWHERE, on EVERYTHING– a car, a person, a forest, the very Earth itself; the crust, mantle, and core, eating away at it until it threw the now-disfigured planet off its axis. We fell out of orbit. The sun got dimmer and the temperature dropped, and when the snows came in, The Gray Tide consumed that too. It took to the air. It became the air. It became the land. It was everything, until all that was left was just a gray, writhing ball cast out into deepest parts of space. And it was somehow STILL GROWING. It would never stop, as it grew so much that it was bigger than the Earth ever was.

From a distance, from outer space, the amorphous blob of James Watsons took on a familiar shape. Like the inkblots Dr. Anne once used to determine my father's emotional stability. Like the black spot on the x-ray of my father's brain itself. Distorted branches reached out through the cosmos, a monstrous space octopus, wrapping itself around the moon and consuming that too. The Gray Tide reached out and ate Venus and Mars and Mercury. It ate the asteroids and the stars and the suns and the planets.

It ate everything.

Until there was only us.

The only survivors left.

And the flimsy, impossible walls that crumbled around us.

114

We were in a refashioned Impossible Room, hundreds of times removed from the original. Rebuilt smaller each time, from the scraps of the former. In essence, we had done the same thing that my father did; we took the materials we had at hand and attempted to offset the future by creating something new. Something that made no sense, if you really thought about it. Something the world would write off as illogical, or pointless, or insane. But we built it anyway.

And in process we somehow shrunk ourselves down. We forced our way into tighter and tighter confines. We discovered how tiny we really were.

115

And so:

These past and the future narratives have finally caught up to one another. There's only one moment left for us to talk about, and that is this moment. The one that I am in. The one that is happening RIGHT NOW in this former building owned by Motherlove Incorporated, in a former city on a former landmass that was a part of a planet formerly known as Earth.

And there went the walls.

Intellectually, we knew they could only protect us for so long. But it was still a shock to watch them go. The final Impossible Room was torn apart on the molecular level, and the materials it was made of were almost instantaneously turned into another few thousand more James Watsons, who in turn pulled the room apart further, repeating the process again and again, until there was nothing left around us but them.

Yes, they surrounded us on all sides, not just to the left and the right, but beneath us and above us too. My brothers. Trillions of them. Maybe ever more than trillions. But who's counting?

My former staff was huddled behind me. Cowering, trembling, fearful. Kelsey and Carol, my wife Helen and her new lover, Einar Kjølaas. It was almost worth it to see the look upon that smug architect's wrinkled face when he realized there was no way out of this situation and that his stupid Impossible

Room wasn't going to save him or anyone else.

The Tide and I stood the exact same height, and they were all built in my exact image, as if I were surrounded by mirrors, although they were naked with gray-tinted translucent skin. A few rouge electrons whizzed around us, like beach balls, before a hand would pop out of the crowd and grab it, pulling it back down into the endless biological mass.

I used to think I was special. I used to think my thoughts and feelings carried more weight than they did. Perhaps it's because my thoughts are the only ones I can hear, and in the cavern of my head things tended to echo. But it didn't really mean anything, objectively speaking. The clock keeps ticking forward:

tick tick tick

And so I removed my clothing. I took off my shirt and pants and undershorts. I got totally naked and I turned around to face the rest of my former subjects. They were sobbing now. Kelsey was slumped over on the floor. Carol audibly sighed as she dropped to her knees. Helen buried her face in Einar Kjølaas's shoulder and he wrapped his skinny arms around her like his body was her jacket. The half-Norwegian architect and I glared at each other malevolently. His chest heaved in and out, but he did not waver, did not cry, did not even blink as all the other James Watsons stepped up behind me like a loyal army behind their general. I guess this was still my kingdom after all.

And we tore the last remaining human beings to shreds and turned them into more of us.

116

And so that's it, everyone.

That's all there is to say.

There's no big moral to this story. No grand proclamations to be made. No lessons to be learned. Or if there were, I guess they've already been distilled and forgotten. In one ear and out the other.

I suppose you could always read this book again, if you really wanted to. Maybe there's some important message you missed. But, honestly, I don't think it will change anything. All these pages have already been written. No matter how many times you look at them, they will always be the same. The same sentences in all the same places, over and over again, one after another, the same words, the same stories, told on a loop, until we reach…

...THE END

Acknowledgments

Thank you to the people who either helped put this book together, listened to me endlessly talk about it, or were just supportive of my writing/art in general. They are, but certainly aren't limited to: Lisa LeStrange, John Skipp, Rose O'Keefe, my mom and dad, Katie McCann, Shawn Vales, Garrett Cook, Jeff Burk, Constance Ann Fitzgerald, Christine Morgan, Michael Allen Rose, Jennifer Robin, John Wayne Comunale, Leza Cantoral, Andrew James Stone, Lee Widener, the Rooster Republic boys, and of course, you people out there who actually pay me money for this bullshit. Thanks!

Danger Slater is the Wonderland-award winning author of *I Will Rot Without You, Puppet Skin, He Digs a Hole,* and other titles. He lives in Portland, OR and has a cat named Bubbles. To his knowledge, he's never been cloned. For updates, you can follow him on Twitter (@Danger_Slater) or just type his name into your little search bar on the computer there. You know how Google works.